Extraterrestrial

Alien Life

Extraterrestrial

Alien Life

By

SIMON KING

CONSCIOUS CARE PUBLISHING PTY LTD

EXTRATERRESTRIAL
Alien Life

National Library of Australia Cataloguing-in-Publication entry:
Author: King, Simon 1950-
Extraterrestrial / by Simon King
ISBN 9780987633767 (Paperback)
Rocky Hudson, Editor.

Printed by Lightning Source
Typeset & cover design by Conscious Care Publishing Pty Ltd

ISBN: 978-0-9876337-6-7

DEDICATION

This book is dedicated to the special fraternity of scientists everywhere who are actively committed to seeking, investigating and resolving the issue of whether life exists beyond our own world, and to the many ufologists who already believe that it does.

It is dedicated to those individuals who have ever sighted or otherwise experienced the phenomenon of aerial craft that are not of this world and/or their occupants who travel in such vessels from beyond our planet.

The book is for those believers among us who, regardless of age, enjoy science fiction in anticipation that it will someday become scientific fact, and for those imaginative individuals who wistfully enjoy the pastime of watching clouds change shape throughout the day. Those people may just occasionally observe a cloud formation resembling a saucer. Is it a flying saucer emerging in the skies, or is it a cloud?

PREFACE

Humans live on a world in a seemingly crowded part of the universe known as the Milky Way Galaxy that is shared by billions of other star systems. We could compare our solar system to a solitary grain of sand on a beach. However, the enormous distances between the planetary systems of these stars can be very difficult to comprehend. So vast are the distances that they are measured in travel time – i.e., *light years* – rather than by the trillions of kilometres actually involved.

We are a fortunate species as intelligent life-forms that thrive on our planet due to a favourable atmosphere, an abundance of water and a relatively compatible climate. Such similar worlds (known as exoplanets) appear to be rare in our part of the cosmos. If there is intelligent life elsewhere, it has not been forthcoming in directly communicating with us.

Extraterrestrial life-forms were once considered to belong solely to the realm of science fiction literature and movies, and this probably has much to do with our own technological development. It is only in the past 60 years humans have progressed to space travel beyond our world, and we still have much to learn about our celestial neighbours.

Our history, as portrayed in the records of various ancient cultures, suggests that we may have been visited in the distant past by life-forms not of this Earth. Often dismissed as mythological gods or legendary beings, these unworldly entities have been etched into our consciousness through many strange pictorial depictions, including hieroglyphs, pictographs and petroglyphs. However, what is apparent is the absence of unequivocal physical evidence of such special visitors – alien artifacts, for example.

From around the middle of the 20th century, a plethora of landings of unidentified flying objects or UFOs were reported from around the planet, and these reports were quickly circulated worldwide by improved telecommunications. Occasionally, selective abductions of people were also reported. Such UFO sightings have drastically declined in recent years and now appear to be comparatively uncommon.

Most incidents were deemed by the relevant investigative authorities to be the result of natural phenomena, or were caused by man-made aerial craft or were simply hoaxes. Many sightings remain inexplicable. The consistency of descriptions of these strange beings and their spacecraft, provided as they were from so many different eyewitnesses, suggests to me that these 'visits' have some merit.

UFO sightings are sometimes dismissed as the advanced technology connected with secretive, experimental military operations. Yet the sheer diversity of 'alien-like spacecraft' sighted would perhaps suggest visitations by different extraterrestrial cultures. Much has been written about why there is rarely any physical proof to substantiate the existence of such life-forms: reasons range from governmental suppression and cover-ups of evidence to elaborate public hoaxes, and this is quite valid. Although given that advanced, potentially superior extraterrestrials are conceivably intent on minimising direct contact with us, perhaps they are just being ultra-cautious.

My book serves to explore these possibilities and examine if these life-forms do actually exist. It considers what they might resemble and their likely intentions, as well as investigates the potential implications of extraterrestrial contact on our own astral journey and ultimate human destiny in the universe.

CONTENTS

LIST OF FIGURES

THE MYSTERIONS

Here lies a man who was not of this Earth

Not Of This Earth, *Sci-Fi Movie (1957)*

Figure 1: The Milky Way Galaxy (© Shutterstock)

EXTRATERRESTRIAL

Have you ever pondered whether there may be intelligent life spread across the vast expanses of our known universe and its countless galaxies? Whether any species of higher intelligence are capable of astral travel to the specific Milky Way Galaxy, comprising our minuscule solar system as well as an estimated 100 to 400 billion stars?[1]

If these enormous numbers are not adequately daunting to the mind, then perhaps the travel involved to merely traverse the Milky Way – an estimated 100,000 -180,000 *light years* – might be a guide.[2]

A light year in astronomy represents the distance light travels in a vacuum in one year, equalling about 9.46 trillion kilometres. For practical purposes, stellar distance is typically quoted in *light years* due to the enormity of physical miles/kilometres between stars and star systems.

Although the Milky Way is a comparatively small and crowded galaxy, the immense plethora of stars and their estimated planetary systems, coupled with the substantial distances to travel, present significant restrictions for any potential space explorer. Hidden away in all this stellar matter is our small inhabited planet with little to attract outside visitors, other than it sustains life.

About seventy percent of the planet's surface is covered in water, resulting in the distinctive 'blue ocean' appearance of Earth when viewed from space. This important element to proliferating 'life' appears relatively uncommon on most other worlds observed from Earth, although the 'life-forms' that possibly exist in those worlds may be nothing like us. Alien species would not necessarily need the same habitable atmosphere and nutrients as humans, and in fact, it is probable they would not.

Another important factor to consider, given the enormity of the universe, is whether our planet may even be discernible on an alien radar. Interestingly, the possibility of a celestial traveller inadvertently discovering our planet is so remote as to be astronomically minimal, given the multitude of other planets and stars crowding our galaxy. Consequently, any visiting outsiders – in all probability – would have come intentionally.

I would predict such space beings to be well advanced in technology and capability, and not necessarily of humanoid shape. We can imagine superior advanced alien cultures may assume a diverse range of forms, as so popularly depicted in science fiction literature and films. From ethereal translucent vapours or changeable shadows, peculiar or exotic creatures to androids, interdimensional beings and pure energy sources – the list of potential alien forms is almost limitless.

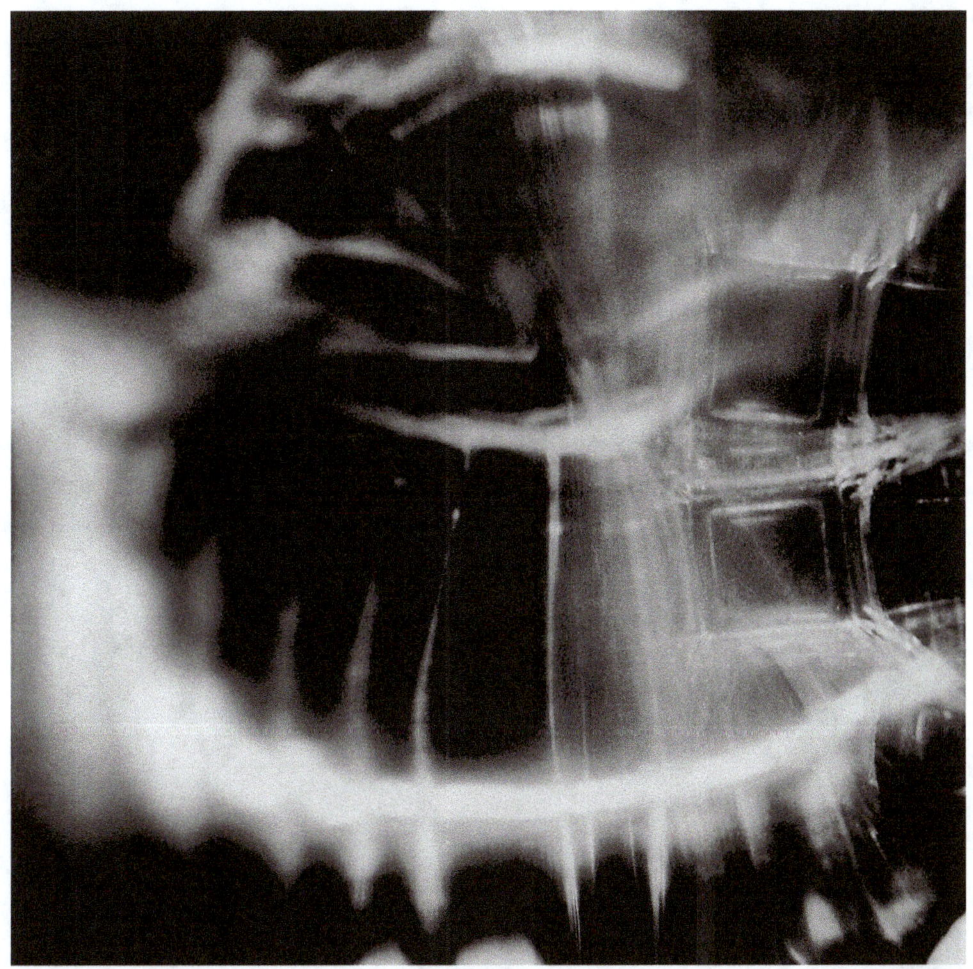

Figure 2: Ethereal Visitor (© Shutterstock)

An alien culture capable of rapidly traversing vast distances safely in space would have to be resilient and highly adaptive. Although variations in the humanoid shape are the most commonly proposed, it is more likely that

EXTRATERRESTRIAL

such travellers are nothing like us in appearance, outlook and nature.

Many science fiction movies have suggested the technological superiority of visiting extraterrestrials is no match for the ingenuity of humankind, or in some cases, the insidiously toxic effect of Earth's airborne bacteria. In many films, the appearance of such aliens is portrayed as an invasion force and lethal threat to *Homo sapiens*, and in others, as a scientific investigation and examination of humans. Neither fictional case augers well for the preservation of our population.

****

Figure 3: Is Anyone Listening? (© Shutterstock)

As Carl Sagan, Professor of Astronomy at Cornell University in New York, succinctly noted in 1972; '…the search for extraterrestrial intelligence to be an exceedingly important one both for science and for society …The best hope for such investigations is NASA's [National Aeronautics and Space Administration] unmanned planetary program and attempts at interstellar radio communication'.[3]

Radio messages about Earth life and culture, or simply seeking a response from any potential alien civilisations, have been broadcast broadly into outer space as well as towards select planetary systems at a carefully planned frequency. These signals have been underway since 1962, but have become very prolific since 1999[4] as a pro-active means of communication.

However, such signals also alert unknown galactic life forces to our specific location in this part of the cosmos. It has been further suggested that should an alien-generated transmission be received, caution should be duly exercised in providing any reply. Given the extraordinary distances to be travelled by such messages, it is highly unlikely that responses would be forthcoming in our lifetimes.

****

For those contemplating the first arrival of extraterrestrials on an alien space craft, the following sobering story from the immensely popular original American television series The *Twilight Zone* (hosted by Rod Serling from 1959 to 1964) recommends due caution.

In a science fiction episode entitled *To Serve Man*, based upon the 1950 short story by Damon Knight and aired on CBS (Columbia Broadcast System) in 1962, the new arrivals promise to share their wonderful technology that will provide limitless energy, cure all disease, convert desert into lush gardens and provide a protective shield around nations to make war obsolete. Paradise has arrived thanks to the aliens' generous benevolence.

As an additional sign of their friendship, the aliens transport humans to the alien home planet as ten year 'exchange groups'. In an effort by humans to eventually translate the alien language, the book acquired from their space craft purporting to be *A Treatise on Serving Humanity* is eventually deciphered to be something far more distasteful, that is, a cookery book. Those humans who travelled to the alien planet never returned, for obvious reasons. Sooner or later, all of us will be on the menu.[5]

'… The cycle of going from dust to desert. The metamorphosis from being the ruler of a planet to an ingredient in someone's soup. It's tonight bill of fare from The Twilight Zone' (Rod Serling's closing narration, 1962).

****

From the myriad of attempts to establish interstellar radio contact with other life forces, only one significant transmission, known as 'the Wow signal', has ever yielded any plausible outcome. Unfortunately, it was transient – being received only once and never repeated. The signal was technically deemed to have originated from a point in space in the direction of Sagittarius by an interstellar radio source of unknown origin rather than as some sort of message; essentially it was a flash of radio energy with no encoded information.[6]

The scientist who detected the unusual signal signature in late 1977 scribed the word 'Wow!' in the margin of the printed signal data, and thus confirmed the important status of such a result.

Despite eliminating other likely sources that may have potentially generated the unique radio signal (including proximity of known planets, asteroids and satellites, space craft and aircraft [which do not transmit on 1,420 megahertz frequency band anyway], complicated astronomical effects or gravitational distortion), no definitive source was plausibly identified.

What makes this particular radio signal of such interest was its transmission on the ideal frequency to be detected with minimal background interference. '…Wow! remains the strongest candidate ever detected for an alien radio transmission'.[7] Such a narrow-band, strong signal with a precise frequency would broadcast for a longer range than say broad-band signal 'noise' constantly generated by stars, and thus would be considered ideal for a means of transmission across the universe.

Despite these considerations, the Wow signal failed to be detected again by

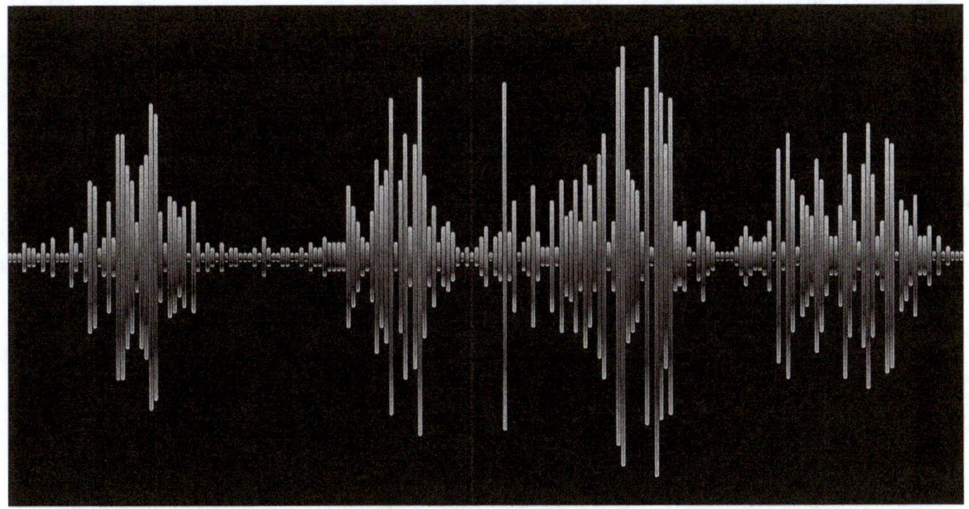

Figure 4: Incoming Transmission (© depositphotos)

a vast number of observations in the same celestial region over years.

If the signal was from an alien source, isn't it likely that it would be repeated far more than once, unless it was strictly a one-off transmission, perhaps from one alien civilisation to another? The cosmic riddle remains unresolved.[8]

****

Probably our best indication of the existence of any extraterrestrial life-forms lies in the surviving artifacts of our ancestors scattered throughout the world – adorning the temples, graphically depicted on rock walls, carved as sculptures, and symbolically represented in massive ornamental civil structures.

Where should we commence such an archaeological search of our most ancient civilisations? How would we decipher between the mythological legends of their respective cultures and the possible presence of alien visitors from the skies?

The golden age of the ancient Maya civilisation, which began around 250 A.D. with the advent of major stone cities and monuments, as well as supreme advances in various cultural and scientific progress, might provide some initial guidance. By 900 A.D., this superior advanced society had effectively dissipated across a massive area occupying southern-eastern Mexico and parts of Central America.

In many ancient cultures, select gods have been symbolically depicted wearing costumes resembling those of astronauts, including bulky space-suits, halo-like helmets (perhaps with an included breathing apparatus), with antennae, and – most importantly – travelling in a flying space chariot or similar airborne craft.

The Maya also produced a rather unusual legendary portrayal of what appears to some to be a spacecraft design, carved into the large stone lid of the sarcophagus of one of their oldest surviving leaders, K'inich Janaab' Pakal I. This highly revered king reigned for an astonishing 68 years until his death in 683 A.D., and consequently was distinguished by a spectacular depiction in his tomb.

The carving was believed by archaeologists to represent the cosmology World Tree (of Creation)[9], depicting Pakal's descent into the underworld along its axis at the moment of his death; the king being positioned in an intermediary space between the heavens and the Mayan underworld.

Alternatively, a further interpretation by other epigraphers who deciphered tomb inscriptions was that of an ascent into the cosmos; '…at the moment of Pakal's resurrection from the underworld and climbing the World Tree towards paradise'. The World Tree was believed by the Maya to have its roots in the underworld, the trunk on the earthly plane and its branches in the heavens.[10]

The conundrum is that the carving superficially appears to illustrate '… the king sitting in a type of cockpit. Could that be … levers in his hands and pedals at his feet? Outside the cockpit is a flame shooting from what appears to be an exhaust?'[11]

Although this latter interpretation of a symbolic carving does not represent the actual mythological portrayal of the dead king, there are still remarkable similarities with a spacecraft, including the seated position of the king who is bending forward, clearly separated from the rear portion of 'the craft', and various apparent pieces of apparatus surrounding him.

Notwithstanding that this specific interpretation has been refuted in detail many times, the symbolic depiction of a flying craft capable of 'ascending to the stars' should raise some plausible questions. How did an ancient civilisation accurately portray such an airborne vessel over 1,300 years ago?

Figure 5: The Ascent (© Shutterstock)

THE BEGINNING

'… it goes against Nature, in a large field to grow only one shaft of wheat, and in the infinite universe only one living world.'[1] [author's emphasis: to suppose that earth is the only populated world in infinite space is as absurd as to believe that in an entire field sown with millet (cereal), only one grain will grow].

Metrodorus of Chios, Greek Philosopher, *On Nature (400 B.C.)*

The controversial subject of initial contact made with beings from other worlds must rest with our most ancient civilisations and their 'gods' who descended from the heavens with cataclysmic powers, including fearsome weapons of mass destruction. The legends detailed by the Sumerians, the world's oldest civilisation, that flourished around 3000 B.C., include half a million years of history, and an account of the arrival of the advanced Anunnaki aliens or 'watchers'.[2]

These were gods with bright and glittering flying machines who were most likely humanoid in appearance.

The creation of a new humanoid species known as the *Adama* (or singular *Adam*) by genetic engineering experimentation on the Earth's existing primitives more than 300,000 years ago was one of the many consequences chronicled about this arrival. Does it mean that this Sumerian 'god' was '… little more than an alien geneticist with obvious human features?'[3] Have

Homo sapiens evolved from one gigantic biological experiment conducted by visiting extraterrestrials?

Mainstream academics and historians disagree with such stories of alien gods from space. It does seem more likely that these ancient texts were an attempt to explain mythical gods in a way that made sense to the Sumerians of those times.

In many religious manuscripts of various ancient cultures, there have been accounts of the wrath of 'the gods'. These included supernormal catastrophic powers capable of eviscerating whole cities and knocking down massive megalithic walls. It has even been written that they '… produced an evil wind that made hair fall out, peeled away the skin, and lead to death by mystic injury'.[4] The givers of knowledge from the skies were also readily capable of destroying civilisations.

Modern scientific advancements have suggested alternative natural causes for these calamitous events or claimed that they were simply mythological sentiments. The debate continues.

The possible existence of extraterrestrial beings and their vivid appearances have been recorded in various pictorial and ancient symbols since the dawn of civilisation. These include Sumerian pictographs, Egyptian hieroglyphics and Mayan ideographs.

Through the ages, images of otherworldly visitors have also been crafted into stone monuments and sculptured carvings. These depictions suggest extraterrestrials possess a dramatic omnipotence.

However, discretionary caution should always be exercised in gauging whether such images generated in ancient times and refreshed by subsequent generations represent 'alien astronauts' or actually reflect iconic mythological spirits of the specific culture.

EXTRATERRESTRIAL

Figure 6: The Mythical One (© Shutterstock)

****

The oldest Australian Aboriginal cave paintings, dated from approximately 3,800 - 4,000 years ago, are typically found in the Kimberley region in the north-west of Australia.

Whether these artistic works are of mythical creative spirits ('Dreamtime stories') and/or are depictions of real life events can be difficult to accurately decipher. What is evident is the great importance and deep religious significance of such cultural images to many generations of indigenous

Australians.

In the specific case of the Wandjina or Wondjina so commonly found in many primitive works of rock art and cave paintings, the preserved features bear a distinctive resemblance to beings not of this physical world – a single class of Creator Being. The Wandjina are cloud and rain spirits that, according to Dreamtime stories, created the landscape and its inhabitants, and continued to influence both of these creations.[5]

These 'sky-beings' or 'spirits from the clouds' descended from the Milky Way Galaxy during Dreamtime and created, taught and served as gods to the Aboriginals.

Wandjina petroglyphs (art requiring the removal of surface layers of rock) depicted in ochre within caves and on rock faces are believed to be the human representation of these spirit ancestors, thus appear in eerie and god-like mythical shapes. They are shown in frontal form, often as a full body but without any anatomical detail. The Wandjina may also be depicted only by head, shoulders and torso, or simply by head and shoulders, possibly extending over an imposing several metres in some artworks.

With their large heads, the Wandjina depictions bear remarkable similarities to the extraterrestrial 'grey aliens' described in various science fiction literature and purported human encounters with such beings. Huge black/dark eyes disproportionate to the nose and face dominate the figure; the nose is slim and almost indistinct, and – most importantly – the mouth and ears are absent.

A humanoid being that appears luminous with dark penetrating eyes and an eerie white face yields a powerful image indeed. However, the predominance of white in these huge ancient paintings may also have a symbolic association with the towering white cumulonimbus clouds that precede the onset of the monsoon season, rather than something 'alien'.[6]

What is of particular interest are the Wandjina's headpiece and a strange garment resembling a small gown (or robe). The elaborate halo-like headdress, with its semicircular band of solid colour or radiating dotted lines, has been described as giving the impression of wearing a helmet or head-

Figure 7: Kimberley Wandjina

dress.[7] Another description is as follows: 'Around the heads of Wandjina are lines or blocks of color, depicting lighting coming out of transparent helmets.'[8]

This headdress is believed to represent both hair and clouds, and the emanating rays to represent the lightning that they control.[9]

The 'rain robe' depicted in some Wandjina paintings has been oddly likened to a spacesuit, although such gown-like garments were customarily worn by ancient seafarers, who may or may not have visited this region of the Indian Ocean in those distant past times.

Do these depictions of mysterious beings give credence to the theory that Wandjinas were extraterrestrial visitors that transcended into myth and legend, or are they meaningful religious representations from civilisations occupying the Kimberley region at least 40,000 years ago?[10]

The answer probably lies within the context of a better comprehension of these spiritual beings from beyond:

> 'The Creator appeared in the form of a Wandjina – mouth and chest shrouded in mist, the head surrounded by circles of lightning and cloud, his gown a curtain of rain – as a Raingod.
>
> You see no mouth, because that is beyond our understanding, our wisdom, our knowledge. It is hidden behind mist, or fog. That mist separates us from the higher levels that we cannot understand [He has no need of a mouth, he sends his thoughts].'[11]

The distinctive features of a Wandjina include the hair, in radial lines. 'The radiating lines from the head are said to represent the lightning that foreshadows the wet season rains.'[12]

All six rings around the head represent clouds and lightning – the first or closest to the head is lightning, the second is low rain-laden clouds, the third is cumulo-nimbus clouds building up to rain, the fourth is cirro-stratus high wind-clouds and the remaining two are a distant cloud bank that flashes lightning, signals the first rain after the Dry [season], respectively.[13]

EXTRATERRESTRIAL

The Wandjina has a line between the eyes rather than a nose to depict where the power flows down from the headdress, and white areas on face and upper chest to represent mists, regions beyond our understanding.[14]

The following poignant quotation from *Yorro Yorro –Spirit of the Kimberley* (1993) provides further insight into the nature of the Wandjina:

> 'Once I was past and future
>> now I am only the present
>> today, the moment
>> and that is hard to bear
>> with no past, no future.'[15]

****

There are many ancient cultures that depict 'Star People' who descended from the heavens in strange powered craft and were subsequently depicted in detailed pictographs (pigmented rock art) or hieroglyphics. These paranormal beings were believed not only to have introduced advanced knowledge and superior capabilities to certain primitive cultures who lacked such understanding, skills and technology, but possibly also became instrumental in such advances.

The world's oldest known human civilisations include the Sumerians in southern Mesopotamia (now modern day southern Iraq), the Harappan culture in the Indus Valley (between north-east Afghanistan, Pakistan and north-west India), and ancient Egypt.

The first two cultures were thriving urban civilisations with suitable sophisticated cities to support their populations. Conversely, Egyptian civilization was actually without a major city until the end of the second millennium B.C., spanning a period of 3,000 years.[16] There are no evident ruins of vast stone cities in Egypt that should signal an advanced civilisation; only massive temples and colossal pyramids remain dotted across the landscape.[17]

Much has been written about the sheer magnitude of the Great Pyramid of Giza in Egypt, supposedly constructed around 4,500 years ago as part of a three pyramid complex. It is 48 storeys high and acts as a permanent large scale geodetic marker, by virtue of its unique location at 0° longitude.[18] 'Indeed, for more than 4,000 years it was known as the largest man-made structure in the world.'[19]

The engineering skills that would be required to prepare and deliver the pyramid's building blocks are advanced and complex, even by today's standards. It is perplexing that this structure could have been created 4,500 years ago.

Figure 8: Great Pyramid of Giza (© Shutterstock)

Hundreds of thousands of massive limestone blocks were generated from nearby solid plateau bedrock to construct the base of the pyramid and interior filling, and further blocks were transported on the Nile River for the exterior facing of the structure. Thousands of enormous and heavier hard stone blocks of granite, often with bevelled faces, were precisely carved (purportedly by manual quarrying) and also transported to the site.

It has been estimated that 2.5 million of these – mostly limestone – blocks were used to construct the structure. This was a period in history when Egyptian culture did not have access to wheels or draught animals to help move the blocks, and there were no hardened iron or steel tools developed or in use to extract and finish the highly abrasive and very hard granite rock.[20] The Egyptians' primitive cutting and impact metal tools were made with relatively soft copper.

The mammoth and complex task of erecting these heavy blocks without access to today's mechanical lifting appliances, such as cranes, hoists or pulleys, is a further technological enigma. They were precisely fitted together with almost no discernible intervening space in the seamless surface, to accurately form a particularly difficult (slightly concave and octagonal) pyramid shape almost 150 metres in height.

Such precise accuracies of the final dimensions of the pyramid are comparable with what is now achieved using modern construction methods and laser leveling.[21]

How was it that the ancient Egyptians were able to deliver such a magnificent and remarkable edifice, considering the primitive tools and construction methods known to be employed in Egypt circa 2500 BCE? According to the Greek historian Herodotus, this astonishing feat of ramp (access) and pyramid construction occupied 30 years with a workforce of 100,000 men.[22]

How could the extraordinary logistics and geo-engineering complexity of this construction be within the capabilities of the Egyptian economy at that time? There are several salient reasons suggesting that the Giza pyramids probably could not have been designed and built by this 'civilisation'.

Ancient Egypt around 2500 BCE was not an advanced civilisation comparable to other such human societies, such as the Sumerians, or the technically superior Roman Empire, neither of which could have built such significant structures using granite blocks.[23]

Cities capable of sustaining such a massive project were not evident in the region at that time. Significantly, there is no indication – other than the pyramids – that even rudimentary 'technological advancements' – such as indoor plumbing, street drainage, and water-delivery systems – were occurring in this same period. These developments were eventually introduced well into the future.[24] It is a conundrum that the society credited with designing and constructing the world's largest artificial edifice at that time, was supposedly unable to readily provide the domestic technology of 'modern conveniences' and planned urban centres to support the project.

Finally, what was the designated purpose for constructing three pyramids in such close proximity on the site?

One suggestion that has been proposed is that the three pyramid complex of Giza may have been designed by an advanced extraterrestrial civilisation to represent very closely the ratios of relative sizes and separation distances of the three inner planets of our solar system, inclusive of Earth[25] – a pyramidal model of these three planets and a sophisticated astronomical set of significant geodetic markers when observed from space.

It must also be assumed that extraterrestrials capable of interstellar travel would be able to harness sufficient energy technology to accurately prepare the pyramid's massive blocks and transport them precisely into the most awkward positions.

Although the ancient Egyptians possessed well established disciplines of engineering, mathematics and science to handle such a complex project, and could accurately identify major stars and use either the positions of stellar bodies or solar observations to orient the pyramids, no records have been found of the design of the Great Pyramid.[26]

Given the magnitude of such a wondrous structure, detailed design plans would have seemed mandatory, yet the only remaining drawings discovered are those for tombs constructed during subsequent dynasties.

SPACECRAFT

I am a leaf on the wind. Watch how I soar.

Hoban 'Wash' Washburne, *Serenity (2005)*

Extraterrestrial pilots do not fly weather balloons or fixed-wing aircraft at high altitude (sometimes mistaken for alien spacecraft in certain circumstances). They do not navigate fast moving spacecraft and missiles, or reflective orbiting artificial satellites, all of which are despatched from Earth and readily visible at night. Satellite re-entries or space junk spectacularly disintegrating in the planet's atmosphere may resemble a descending alien craft, but extraterrestrial pilots are not responsible for this either.

It is also unlikely that aliens could control peculiar bulbous or unusual lenticular cloud formations resembling spaceships, such as flying saucers for example. Yet all have been incessantly reported to various government authorities as unidentified flying objects (UFOs) in the past.

UFO (or 'UFOB') is not the only term to describe such strange phenomena, although it is the most popular. The phrase UFOB was defined in 1953 as 'any airborne object which by performance, aerodynamic characteristics,

Figure 9: *Altocumulus Standing Lenticularis* (© Shutterstock)

or unusual features, does not conform to any presently known aircraft or missile type, or which cannot be positively identified as a familiar object'.[1]

If appropriate investigation determines the object to be '… something beyond the bounds of recognized natural phenomena … it may be considered an *extraordinary flying object* [EFO]. Even more startling, it might be called an *alien flying object* [AFO] meaning a vehicle constructed by alien intelligence'.[2]

There are innumerable meteorological phenomena occurring in our atmosphere. The optical illusions created by bizarre cloud formations and freakish combinations of waning sunlight and water vapour/ice crystals near twilight, night shining (*noctilucent*) effects, or colourful glowing iridescence generate many images confusing to the human eye.

Round or oval lens-shaped cloud or 'lenticularis' can often be quite elongated with very distinguished boundaries that may resemble a smooth saucer-like or disk shape. As such clouds remain relatively stationary, they can

Figure 10: Spaceships of the Skies (© Shutterstock)

Figure 11: Solitary Flying Saucer (© Shutterstock)

Figure 12: The Mothership (© Shutterstock)

form unique large-scale 'standing' shapes, much like a hovering spaceship or even multiple level spacecraft.

This unusual appearance is further enhanced when they appear to dissipate quickly with rapidly changing air patterns, providing the atmospheric illusion of a spacecraft 'speeding away'.[3]

The rare occurrence of strange lenticular clouds is usually but not always related to high altitude mountainous terrain rather than low-lying or flat terrain. Hence their odd bulbous appearance will be unfamiliar to many.

A scarf or cap cloud is a small horizontal lenticular cloud that can hover above an isolated mountain peak, culminating in the appearance of a 'shroud' that is sometimes mistaken for a flying saucer or saucers, given the right prevailing optical conditions.

Such cloud forms when a layer of moist air rises above the mountain and sinks after passing this obstacle. A 'standing wave' is created in the lee side of the slope where moisture condenses to form what appears to be a hover-

Figure 13: Cap Cloud (© Shutterstock)

ing cloud resembling a near-stationary spacecraft. If this cloud should also be slightly inclined due to the downward flow of the leeside air, this would enhance the appearance of a spacecraft hovering.[4]

Given such a diversity of atmospheric conditions and realistic cloud shapes, it would not be unexpected that some may be potentially confused with alien spacecraft. There is also an array of natural celestial phenomena that have been mistakenly identified as alien airships, including transient comets, disintegrating meteors in our atmosphere and even the brightest of stars and planets visible from Earth.

****

Astronomers are continually vigilant in their systematic optical and photometric observations for possible sightings of unusual or unidentified bright objects traversing our solar system, and considerably further afield in our galaxy, although such sightings are almost always explicable.

It is probably salient to mention that the advanced technology of any alien civilisation capable of interstellar travel of massive distances is highly likely to include anti-detection or stealth devices to cloak their spaceships. This would then make visual and radar detection extremely difficult, regardless of day or night conditions.

Appraisal of reported 'spacecraft' sightings in the modern era initially commenced in 1947 with the United States Air Force official project named 'Sign' to investigate such UFO occurrences. This was subsequently replaced by 'Project Grudge' in 1949 and ultimately as 'Project Blue Book', which was to last 17 years until being terminated in 1969.

Despite the massive number of UFO reports accumulated between 1947 and 1969 (12,618), only 701 incidents – less than 6 per cent – could not be satisfactorily explained by astronomical, meteorological or artificial (man-made) causes, despite stringent analysis.[5,6]

This is perhaps simplifying the scientific analysis of the collected data to an extent, given the era involved operation of experimental, high technology military aircraft during the Cold War period that did not warrant any such close scrutiny or detrimental reporting.

Furthermore, the 701 unexplained unidentified flying objects listed in Project Blue Book may have only represented a portion of such cases, for a diversity of complex reasons. One estimate provided in 1968 suggests that an estimated 30-40 per cent of the total reports accumulated could still remain unexplained, representing roughly between 3,000 to 5,000 cases (McDonald 1968[7]), and that the overall tally of 12,618 of UFO reports was closer to 15,000.[8]

Notwithstanding confidential matters of national security, the official findings of the studies overwhelmingly concluded in part that '… There was no evidence indicating that sightings categorized as "unidentified" were extraterrestrial vehicles'.[9]

****

As with any scientific investigation and analysis, attention to detail is crucial in determination of the eventual findings.

EXTRATERRESTRIAL

Consider the well-publicised supposed UFO sighting occurring in Ohio in April 1966, when local police officers spotted a metallic, disc-shaped silvery object with a very bright light [to make your eyes water] emanating from its underside, at about 1000 feet (305 metres) in altitude about 05:00 am one morning. The object was followed/pursued for about 30 minutes over 85 miles (137 km), with it sometimes descending as low as 50 feet (15 metres).[10,11]

The resultant findings were that the officers had initially been chasing a communications satellite and then the planet Venus refracted through fog.

On the opposite side of the world in the previous year, in the early hours on 3rd September 1965, a rather different flying object was observed at different times by several people around Exeter and Kensington in New Hampshire, England.

These included motorists, a hitchhiker and police officers, who variously described the bizarre vehicle as ' … like a rugby ball viewed from the side, with five extraordinarily bright, pulsating red lights or "windows" along its side …the lights were in a line at about a sixty-degree angle… only one light would be on at a time .. pulsating one, two, three, four, five, four, three, two, one … formed a distinct halo-effect around the object making it difficult to perceive the precise outline of the larger body…'[12,13]

The red light emanating from the object was painful to watch due to its extreme brilliance.

The object made no sound, floated and frequently hovered at shallow heights after rising from behind trees, and was observed accelerating and stopping at rates difficult to track visually. With an estimated width of approximately 80-90 feet (24-27 metres), this substantial craft reportedly 'chased and swooped' two motorists on that evening.

This was a very well documented encounter with the eventual tangible explanation only provided forty-five years later.

The flying object may have been a U.S. Air Force KC-97 refuelling tanker plane operating in the same area that evening as part of a scheduled two day airborne training exercise. Such a plane displays five red light sequencing and has a reflective fuel boom which when lowered could display this illumination at the sixty-degree angle estimated by a witness. It is also fitted with three high intensity lights on the underbelly for night refuelling.[14]

The KC-97 is a slow-moving aircraft that requires long circuits of the rendezvous area to refuel other planes, and with its fuel boom lowered, appears to flutter or hover in the air. Such a slow-moving refuelling process between two planes 'jockeying' into position, and the extreme brightness of lighting could also provide quite an illusionary effect observed from the ground.[15]

Given these remarkable similarities, it was probably not an alien spacecraft after all.

****

However, the unidentified flying object observed by three people in broad daylight on the morning of 23rd April 1954 in Pittsfield, Maine, USA re-

Figure 14: Simulated Bright Flying Object (© depositphotos)

mains inexplicable. The experience only lasted four minutes but has been aptly described in the Project Blue Book Unknowns (Case Number 2974):

'… a silver circular saucer-shaped object with a dome half the size of the base that was the source of constantly flashing brilliant light, making a loud sound like a swarm of bees, which hovered at about 70° azimuth without tilting, flew horizontally with a whirlwind effect and cold air that moved stones underneath its path, then it rose vertically at 30° azimuth without tilting until out of sight'.[16]

Remarkably, at dusk on the following day at Hartland, Maine, approximately 11 miles (18 kilometres) away, a solitary witness reported sighting a very large silver oblong object stationary on the horizon. It also had a dome on top and flashing light inside this dome, and after 15 minutes climbed straight up [vertically] and disappeared. No sound or exhaust trail was evident. (Case No 2975)

****

For some acclaimed scientific specialists who have been extensively exposed to sightings of UFOs and are experienced in the identification of their various engineering and operational characteristics, the matter is beyond reasonable doubt. As Dr Bruce Rodgers, Professor of Mechanical Engineering acknowledged:

'There is much that is mystifying about UFOs, and woefully little information about them. But, there is one thing about which there can be no doubt. Whoever builds and operates these vehicles possess a technology incredibly advanced beyond anything known on our planet.'[17]

Aeronautics specialist Dr Paul Hill has comprehensively investigated these phenomena, including his personal sightings over many years, and developed theories on how such craft might function. He also appreciated that such advanced technology exceeded the capability of humans, and thus were of extraterrestrial origins.

His protocol in designating such unusual crafts as *unconventional objects*

(UO) rather than as UFOs was to eliminate the perception that they had to fly through our atmosphere, which they do not use for any support nor locomotion, unlike our aircraft. Interestingly, Dr Hill was also responsible for officially coining the term UFO to replace the words flying saucers.[18]

WINGLESS SHAPES AND NOCTURNAL LIGHTS

The night creeps in by subtle degrees while a show of fierce colors attracts and distracts me. I look up, suddenly aware of remote lights scattered overhead. I gasp as the last streak of fire dies on the horizon, and I comprehend it all too late. That crafty, dark night has swallowed my world whole.

Henry David Thoreau, *Smile Anyway (2015)*

'The total number of stars in the sky is roughly the same as the total number of grains of sand on *all* Earth's beaches, put together.'[1]

If alien spacecraft actually exist and have ventured into our solar system from any of the plethora of star systems beyond our skies, then the type of spaceships may also be diverse.

Of the various sightings of unidentified flying objects not directly attributable to astronomical, meteorological, artificial (man-made) or other Earthbound sources, inclusive of hoaxes, there appears one relatively common

Figure 15: Multiple Star Systems (© Shutterstock)

factor shared by many of these reports – and that is the shape of such spacecraft.

The most prolific design appears to be geometrical, such as a disc (flat, domed or double domed, hemispherical), a rounded sphere, an egg shape (elliptical or oval-shaped object), a cylinder or a triangular pyramid. These types of shape provide aerodynamic contours for space travel. Almost all models are wingless or have modified ancillary winglets.

Of course, the propulsion means for interstellar travel of such vessels remains unconfirmed and thus subject to supposition. However, the physical shapes observed suggest high technology streamlined spacecraft emanating from very advanced alien culture(s).

Terrestrial aircraft, on the other hand, rarely deviate into 'alien or unconventional designs' merely because of the aerodynamic instability exhibited by such configurations and the limitations of our present technological capability.

Advanced military aircraft such as the Stealth fighter may indeed have an unconventional look '… but for the most part, advanced aircraft maintain a fairly traditional appearance …'[2]

Alien craft have commonly been described by observers as having a 'shiny metallic or a light reflecting surface'. They appear to be made of a smooth, translucent materials, which have not been confirmed to be metals or synthetics with properties common to our world. This is probably because physical materials suitable for scientific examination have yet to be retrieved from such vessels.

These vessels are fascinating not just for their sophisticated physical shapes, but for their extraordinary capability to adjust their direction of movement and speed.

Figure 16: Out of this World (© Shutterstock)

Various witness observations over time describe extremes of acceleration and shifts in direction, sometimes without any obvious reason or purpose. These qualities would suggest these vessels can also readily traverse vast expanses of space in nominal time.

'Speeds [of unconventional flying objects] to about 9,000 miles per hour (mph) have been measured by radar at 60,000 feet (18,300 m) altitude … by radar near 18,000 feet (5,500 m) altitude … '[3] This equates to astronomical flight speeds of more than 14,000 kilometres per hour (kph) even at significant altitudes.

In comparison, most of the world's fastest military jets only achieve top speeds around 2,000 mph to 2,600 mph (3,200 - 4,200 kph). The exception is the X-43 experimental unmanned hypersonic aircraft. This was developed by NASA as part of its Hyper-X program and is the fastest aircraft on record, with a top speed of an incredible Mach 9.6 or approximately 7,000 mph.[4]

Man-made craft are not yet capable of sustaining these high speeds over extended periods or while conducting extreme manoeuvres. This would be an entirely different proposition, particularly given the tremendous impact of Earth's gravitational forces on such aircraft.

UFOs have been observed at various altitudes completing sudden reversals of direction (180 degree turnaround) at speed, achieving outstanding acceleration from a stationary start in any direction, and performing a range of other fantastic positional manoeuvres that are just not possible with current terrestrial aircraft.

The alien propulsion systems capable of generating such phenomenal flight patterns and lightning speeds whilst easily defying our gravity field are probably quite diverse, and not the product of Earth-technology (diesel, jet or nuclear).

There are several scientific possibilities that could explain such alien performance, ranging from distorting stellar and planetary gravitational fields and converting the gravity into useful energy for propulsion uses, force field/beam propulsion inclusive of negative gravity or other as yet unknown mechanisms for cosmic energy conversion.[5]

A review of reported sightings conducted in 1947 by the intelligence and technical divisions of the US Air Materiel Command at their headquarters at Wright Field in Ohio determined that these flying objects were characterised by extreme rates of climb [and] manoeuvrability, with a general lack of noise and an absence of trail (except when operating under high performance).[6] With estimated level flight speeds above 300 knots (556 kph), occasional formation flying (varying from three to nine objects), and evasive behaviour when sighted or contacted by friendly aircraft and radar, they were considered to be a controlled craft.[7]

Figure 17: Simulated Formation Flying of Models (© depositphotos)

One of the strangest encounters involving a wingless UFO occurred in April 1980 and was also possibly the only documented case of a military pilot attacking such a craft using his jet's weapons. The Peruvian air force pilot had been alerted to a mysterious silvery balloon-shaped craft hovering at around 600 metres altitude near the end of the runway to his base.

The craft was within a highly sensitive military area and did not respond to any communications, prompting the pilot to engage the airborne intruder. Although firing a fearsome volley of 60 rounds of 30mm calibre shells directly at the craft, it had no effect whatsoever, as if the shells had been absorbed.

Instead, the UFO commenced a prolonged and elusive game of cat-and-mouse, accelerating upwards each time the fighter jet approached and was about to fire again. These manoeuvres lasted only about 22 minutes and ultimately reached a staggering altitude of 19,200 metres, but were long enough for the fighter pilot to gain a detailed view of the balloon-like craft.

It was about ten metres in diameter with a shiny, cream-coloured dome on top 'similar to a light bulb cut in half', with a wider circular metallic silver base. The craft lacked all the typical components of aircraft, having no apparent wings, antennae, exhausts or visible propulsion system.

Perhaps the most definitive element to this unique encounter was that after the jet fighter returned to base, low on fuel and having been unsuccessful in disabling the craft, this 'object of unknown origin' simply remained in the same position for another two hours, visible to all on the base.[8]

****

The other unidentified flying objects that are most commonly described are 'sharply defined luminous objects'. They are observed as small anomalous balls or spheres of bright light in the night sky at a distance. Atmospheric effects such as electrical ball and bead lightning and other natural phenomena, including meteoroid fireballs and swamp/marsh gas, have been attributed to such sightings, yet in certain select cases, they remain inexplicable.

Nocturnal lights may also be attributable to terrestrial aircraft, passing satellites or similar craft, except for some very salient differences. Reports from various witnesses over the years confirm that such 'lights' not only change directions and altitude in flight, often in radical moves, but can accelerate at incredible speeds and vanish. In one specific case over England in 1956, a UFO was monitored by radar to be travelling at about 3,000 miles per hour, or an astounding 4,800 kph, at low altitude.[9]

UFOs known as 'shapeshifters' may be such an example of this phenomenon. Shapeshifting objects have been occasionally reported by eyewitnesses as spacecraft that alter their configuration in flight or sometimes generate up to several smaller 'glowing spheres' that exit the vessel in different directions. These smaller entities travel at incredible speeds and can rapidly alter direction and altitude, or simply hover above the ground. They may also return to the mother ship.

Some unidentified nocturnal bright lights also have a propensity to change colour and light intensity, with reported instances of drastic variations depending upon the object's manoeuvre or positioning. Rarely is noise ever detected from such objects and on occasion, there have been sightings of multiple lights travelling independently of each other.

It is unlikely such mysterious sightings were actually experimental military aircraft, given that 'even the most modern aircraft cannot make ninety-degree turns or ascend out of sight within mere seconds ...' and such test flights would not be performed over large population areas where they could be readily scrutinised.[10]

Military 'stealth' aircraft are known as shadowcraft because they remain virtually undetectable to radar systems, appearing as an object of substantially smaller size, such as a large bird for example. The stealth technology also works to avoid detection of the shadowcraft by reduction of infrared (heat) emission and reflection of visible light.

For obvious security reasons, such jet aircraft may operate in the dark to further minimise visual detection. Therefore, a UFO that has been reported as 'brightly illuminated and travelling quite slowly' in the night is unlikely to be a shadowcraft.

A comprehensive review in 2000 by the British Ministry of Defence (made public in 2006) of a statistically representative group of reports received of 'unidentified aerial phenomena' (UAP) between 1987 and 1997, coupled with an overview of all reports over 30 years, identified some interesting findings concerning these strange occurrences.[11]

In particular, the presence of some mysterious brightly coloured, fast-moving lights sometimes described as shapes and occasionally reported with

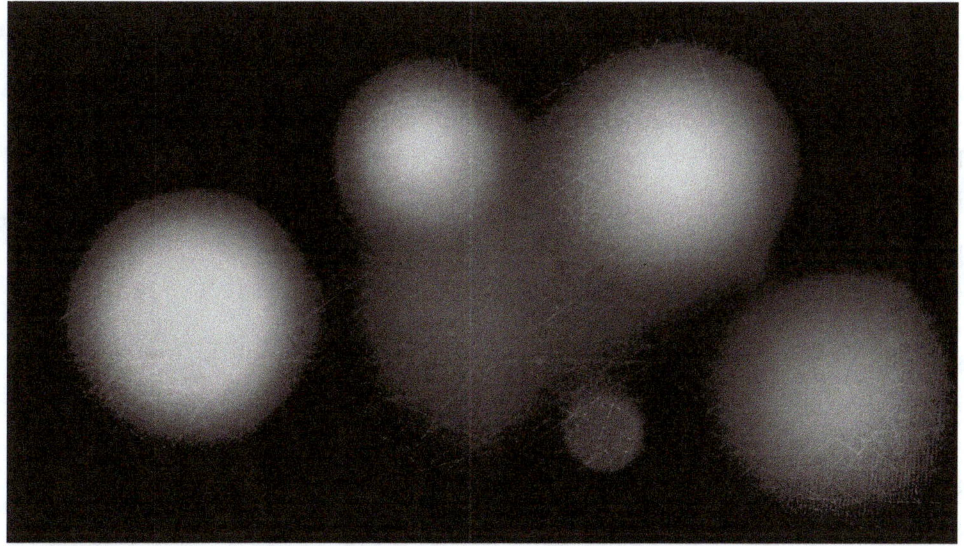

Figure 18: Nocturnal Lights (© Shutterstock)

sound and smell may be the result of 'several types of rarely encountered natural events' creating electrically-charged plasma fields in our skies under the right conditions:

> '… the events are almost certainly attributable to physical, electrical and magnetic phenomena in the atmosphere, mesosphere and ionosphere. They appear to originate due to more than one set of weather and electrically-charged conditions and are observed so infrequently as to make them unique to the majority of observers. There seems to be a strong possibility that at least some of the events may be triggered by meteor re-entry, the meteors neither burning up completely nor impacting as meteorites, but forming buoyant plasmas [fireballs]'.[12]

Electrically-charged plasma [hot ionised gas] created in our skies can be a complex topic and such pre-emptive conditions required for plasma formation are subject to variations. These complexities can create additional 'mysterious' effects with respect to their visual detection.

> '… As an electrically-charged, but not ionised, gaseous mass,

> this may be either visible to the eye but not to radar sensors; or
> fully ionised and visible to both'.[13]

Occasionally and perhaps exceptionally, the field between certain charged buoyant objects in loose formation forms an area often triangular in shape which does not reflect light. This phenomenon by such an unexplained energy field creates a black triangle that actually refracts light, described by observers as a black triangular 'craft' up to hundreds of feet in length.[14]

An additional element to such 'buoyant plasma formation' that may not always be detected by radar is that being in close proximity to such charged masses [energy field] may also adversely affect a vehicle, effectively disabling it for a period. It seems far more than simple nocturnal lights in the sky.

More recently, the Advanced Aviation Threat Identification Program operated by the U.S. Defense Intelligence Agency which began in 2007 and ended in 2012 also studied and investigated UAP, specifically for their potential as a threat to national security. This involved seeking to identify what had been reported or witnessed in order to determine if such information presented a potential threat to the nation.

The former director of the program, who resigned from active service in 2017, subsequently recounted his personal belief about the investigatory work:

> '…These aircraft -- we'll call them aircraft -- are displaying
> characteristics that are not currently within the US inventory nor
> in any foreign inventory that we are aware of … they identi-
> fied 'anomalous' aircraft that were 'seemingly defying the laws
> of aerodynamics' … Things that don't have any obvious flight
> services, any obvious forms of propulsion, and maneuvering
> in ways that include extreme maneuverability beyond, I would
> submit, the healthy G-forces of a human or anything biological
> …'[15]

This is an interesting perspective on the ageless pursuit of identifying whether other life-forms are in the air around our world.

WINGLESS SHAPES AND NOCTURNAL LIGHTS

American author Jeffrey Allan Danelek provides a fascinating commentary on such prolific UFO sightings and the apparent extraterrestrial origin of such spacecraft (2008):

> 'The wide range of UFO configurations, then, would suggest that Earth is being studied by a number of different races – only a few of which apparently choose to interact with us – or that there are just a few races that have a vast array of different craft at their disposal.'[16]

LANDINGS

These beings, with soaring imagination, eventually flung themselves and their machines into interstellar space.

Carolyn Porco, *Planetary Scientist*

If any unidentified flying objects are of extraterrestrial origin and have landed on our planet, what is the core purpose for such exploratory visits and, more importantly, should we be worried?

There is a diversity of alternative thoughts concerning such intentions, ranging from eventual exploitation of our natural resources, inclusive of the Earth's copious water, mineral reserves and other energy raw materials, enslavement of the human population or worse, to more benign purposes, such as alien colonisation of the new planet, or to research and learn more about our civilisation without direct intervention.[1]

These subjective viewpoints rely upon some basic assumptions that an extraterrestrial life form would be interested in a planet with an oxygen-rich atmosphere already teeming with microscopic life that continues to contribute to this atmosphere.

Alternatively, it may only serve as a minor habitation inconvenience to such aliens. If such planets are common in the universe, or conversely are relatively rare, the presence of intelligent life-forms such as humans may be a decisive factor in whether they will land here.

Given that *Homo sapiens* are organic and born of 'flesh and bone', thus relatively susceptible to injury, disease and eventual death, our fragile species may be somewhat rare throughout the known universe. Additionally, we are yet to travel beyond our small solar system in passenger spaceships, nor have we developed stellar craft capable of planetary travel faster-than-the-speed-of-light of about 300,000 kilometres per second. It would not be unreasonable to assume there remains quite a journey ahead in terms of our technological development.

Alien landings for the purposes of suitable scientific research and comprehension of our life forms could be another likely outcome.

Of the very few select witnessed landings or take-offs reported within a comprehensive sample of more than 1,700 useful UFO cases (1947 – 1969) taken from Project Blue Book records,[2] there are some surprising commonalities across several years of separate sightings.

Witnesses variously reported compact and distinctive landing indentations or less defined ground impressions, usually up to a nominal 20 centimetres depth, dependent upon the vessel size and shape. The ground surface remaining after take-off was covered by scorch marks, patches of singed grass, or larger areas – approximately matching the diameter of the craft – exhibiting signs of intense heat.

Decaying radioactivity levels well in excess of typical 'background' values for radiation (i.e. the value not resulting from deliberate introduced natural or artificial radiation sources at the particular location) were measured at three of these sites. During some landing or take-off activities, any terrestrial vehicle in reasonable proximity also reportedly experienced interruption to electrical power for the petrol engine, headlights, radio, as well as damage to the battery. Diesel engines did not appear affected.

In yet other reported cases, no trace of disturbed ground was evident or located where a vessel had left the ground. UFOs have been reported as simply hovering at or immediately above ground surface, which may be a possible explanation for the lack of such physical traces.

Another common feature of reported landings, in cases where 'inhabitants' of the craft had been sighted, albeit from quite a distance, was their remarkably small size, estimated at about three feet or one metre in height. These very short beings were described as having humanoid bodies but lacked discernible facial features. In one unusual account, the UFO occupants were heard communicating in piercing and high-pitched voices similar to those of children playing.

For the sceptics, it can be relatively easy to dismiss such isolated cases as potentially elaborately contrived hoaxes or possibly the plausible results of some rare natural event, such as extraordinary atmospheric electrical phenomena in the region.

What cannot be so easily dismissed is that in these few cases, reports indicated the observed inhabitants departed in each spacecraft once detected, thereby avoiding any direct contact with humans.

This may seem an unusual element to a possible 'extraterrestrial' landing, unless it is viewed in the context of a number of practical possibilities, ranging from the need to maintain strict secrecy about their presence to enforced avoidance of contact with another intelligent species.

The American astronomer, cosmologist, astrophysicist, astrobiologist and popular science author Carl Sagan made the following astute observation in 1994: 'Our planet is a lonely speck in the great enveloping cosmic dark. In our obscurity, in all this vastness, there is no hint that help will come from elsewhere to save us from ourselves.'[3] Perhaps that is also the way any such extraterrestrial visitors would prefer it.

****

Spacecraft landings for purposes of scientific research on distant planets can be found in various popular science fiction magazine stories circulating since the late 1940s. The visits can also be particularly brief in the right circumstances.

Take the tale of an Earth spaceship that ventures to a planet in a remote sector of the galaxy, involving an extended journey of several months. Others have landed to conduct scientific research in past years but never returned. This spaceship arrives to discover the unexplored planet is covered entirely in dense vegetation with virtually nowhere to safely land the craft.

Eventually, a suitable site apparently cleared of vegetation is detected and a landing is completed. It is only then that the two astronauts on board realise that the surrounding vegetation has been cut-down in one extensive swath extending for at least an estimated one kilometre radius. Both leave the vessel and commence walking towards the untouched vegetation along the perimeter of the landing site.

In the distance, dark clouds form, indicating a storm may develop, as the astronauts reach the forested perimeter after several minutes of brisk walking. They are now about 200 metres from their spacecraft. The distant thunderstorm starts moving rapidly in their direction so they wisely decide to return to the safety of their ship without delay. However, this is no ordinary thunderstorm.

Once inside, the astronauts observe the approaching maelstrom as it unleashes a continuous torrent of massive hailstones the size of cannonballs, smashing to the ground and flattening all vegetation in its path. The air is thick with these destructive demolition projectiles.

Now it becomes evident to the crew why the surrounding vegetation at the landing site had been so effectively flattened

In sheer panic, they decide to abort the mission and depart as quickly as possible just as the storm reaches the spaceship. Fifteen minutes later, the exploratory craft that ventured so far across the galaxy is reduced to pulverised minute fragments of metal and scrap, as were the previous spaceships that never returned. A planet with a very dangerous weather system for any potential future explorers.

Figure 19: Alien Storm (© Shutterstock)

****

It is not easy to provide substantive, readily verifiable proof about extraterrestrial spacecraft which may have landed on our planet.

For the vast majority of recorded cases worldwide, proof has largely relied upon visual or photographic observations of the unusual phenomena and the presence of independent, credible witnesses, such as government officials, commercial pilots and astronauts. Physical evidence is relatively rare, as these spacecraft do not tend to leave any physical traces of alien activity.

The exception to this matter are unexplained ground disturbances at sites where such landings have been observed. This provides the rare opportunity for scientists to conduct analytical evaluation and independent corroboration of such physical proof.

There is probably no better documented proof than the case of the 'glowing scorched landing ring' that occurred around 7 pm on 2nd November 1971 in Delphos, Kansas USA.

The appearance of a brightly glowing, mushroom-domed, disk-shaped object that had descended almost to the ground with a rumbling machinelike noise was first witnessed by a sixteen-year-old boy on his family farm.[4] The object, with a diameter of six to eight feet (1.8 -2.4 metres), was entirely enveloped in a bright glow, making it difficult to describe anything other than its shape in detail.[5]

As the object hovered immediately above ground level under a tree 75 feet (23 metres) away, the witness noted that there was also a bright glow between the object and the ground below. This glow was so brilliant that the witness was momentarily blinded.[6]

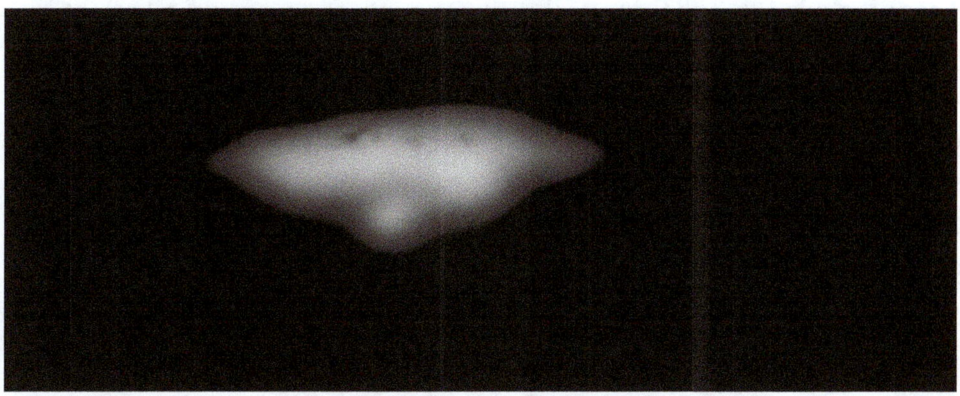

Figure 20: The Descent (© Shutterstock)

EXTRATERRESTRIAL

As the object ascended into the night sky, the teenager's parents also witnessed it departing in a southerly direction. Around 7:30pm in Minneapolis, 10 miles south of Delphos, a further witness observed a bright light descending in the night sky and subsequently reported the matter to police.[7]

Interestingly, the ground below where the object had been hovering bore a remarkable 'scorched' ring that remained intact on the ground, and was to intrigue scientists for over forty years. The shape of this landing ring was elongated in the direction of the prevailing wind that night, providing further confirmation of its formation.

Most importantly, the ring was glowing brightly and continued to glow the following morning, despite rain during the night. This glow had also been evident on the leaves of the nearby trees where the descent had occurred. Unlike the surrounding soil, the ring remained impervious to water, including winter snow, and almost four years later, the soil was photographed as having turned a whitish colour.[8]

When the glowing ring was touched on that night, it had a strangely numbing anaesthetic effect on the fingers, and the soil was described as being '… like a slick crust, as if the soil was crystallized'.[9]

Scientific analysis over the ensuing years, in the early 1970s and subsequently in the late 1990s, discovered some astonishing facts about the scorched soil. Its characteristics were quite different to the undisturbed ground nearby.

These included that the ring soil was not exposed to a physical effect like a high temperature, (which in the author's opinion could reasonably be expected from scorch marks by spacecraft manufactured on Earth). Another interesting outcome to possibly explain the physical effects that were suffered by the witnesses was that 'free oxalic acid had been deposited in the soil' and combined with calcium already present in the ground to generate skin and eye irritants. This process may have possibly also caused the glowing effect of the ring soil and the luminescence on nearby trees.[10,11]

The profound water-repellent nature of soil samples collected from within the ring were found to be due to the presence of an unusual highly water-soluble organic compound that would not have been produced by fungi (naturally present in most soils).

Although the exact physical constitution of soil compound could not be fully identified, it was potentially chemiluminescent (emission of light as result of a chemical reaction), with the following conclusion: 'The hovering object of presently unknown origin appears to have contained within its periphery an aqueous solution of an unstable compound whose likely sole function would be light emission … some of the solution was deposited into the ground while the object positioned itself under a tree…'[12]

Figure 21: Minimal Ground Disturbance (© Shutterstock)

We may never know the purpose of the landing that possibly left the scorched ring in the ground, but two interesting aspects to this event subsequently surfaced. They concerned the original witness and the dog who had accompanied him.

EXTRATERRESTRIAL

The teenager revealed a missing period of time in his memory, a period between trying to gain a better view of the bright flying object and when it eventually departed. The teenager's dog also was later found to have a long metallic implant lodged inside its snout, which was surgically removed and then retained by the witness.[13]

 Both are enigmas that have yet to be resolved.

Scientists have noted that hovering flying saucers above ground (same purpose as landing) sighted elsewhere at times '… form chemically and physically altered annular rings in the earth itself … called "saucer rings" … leave evidence of charred roots or wilted plants … if low-hovering, sometimes swirl down "grass rings" …'[14].

Perhaps most importantly, such craft do not appear to radiate intense heat from their surfaces or in their surrounds, and at night can be observed with a halo of neon-like, solid-colour luminescence emanating from an envelope of air around the object's surface, thus obscuring the craft.[15]

This indistinct definition around the craft's edges by the glowing halo (ion sheath) provides the temporary illusion that the flying saucer is a different shape, particularly below the vessel.

VISITORS

It was just a colour out of space – a frightful messenger from unformed realms of infinity beyond all Nature as we know it; from realms whose mere existence stuns the brain and numbs us with the black extra-cosmic gulfs it throws open before our frenzied eyes.

H.P. Lovecraft, *The Colour Out of Space (1927)*

If extraterrestrial visitors from other worlds or dimensions have arrived on our planet, they must have developed supreme camouflage to blend so meticulously into human society. To propose that such aliens could live among us and survive biologically in our physical atmosphere by subterfuge and intricate deception is difficult to justify scientifically.

Even if they appeared externally identical to us in every way, their internal physiology would almost certainly not be the same – for example, they might have multiple hearts, an extra lung, different organs.

There have been innumerable reported UFO events investigated for such life-forms since the late 1940s, and high level governmental studies and further investigations have been conducted. So where are these aliens if they exist, and why is it so difficult to recognise such visitors?

The obvious conclusion is that such beings largely resemble ourselves, al-

EXTRATERRESTRIAL

though this is a rather simplified and almost presumptive response.

They may be carbon-based life-forms with soft bodies and liquid for

Figure 22: Possible Interdimensional Life (© Shutterstock)

'blood' to transfer nutrients to all body cells. Short humanoid beings with arms and legs, an upright stance and '…a skeleton to bear the body and probably eyes, a lung and a mouth'[1] have been described from isolated UFO incidents.

Scientific conjecture hypothetically suggests such life-forms could be entirely different from us: '… non-cellular plasma-based life-forms, or huge single-cell organisms, or even life living in two dimensions or … in parallel Universes'.[2]

Unfortunately, we lack any concrete scientific evidence to confirm these possibilities. As a consequence, our limited knowledge of any such probable alien existence tends to be based upon our own evolutionary history and the known universe. It is only supposition to suggest what we cannot confirm with examples of physical proof.

Suffice to say, the best educated guess is that any eventual extraterrestrial visitor would not be humanoid at all and would probably lack most facial features, excluding perhaps eyes. It would be realistic to anticipate such life-forms would certainly be 'very alien indeed' and more suited to their home environment than to our terrestrial biosphere.

Such a world may be supporting life in a totally different atmosphere, one without prolific nitrogen, oxygen and water, as well as other essential factors (energy, nutrients and minimal radiation levels) we require for our ongoing habitation.

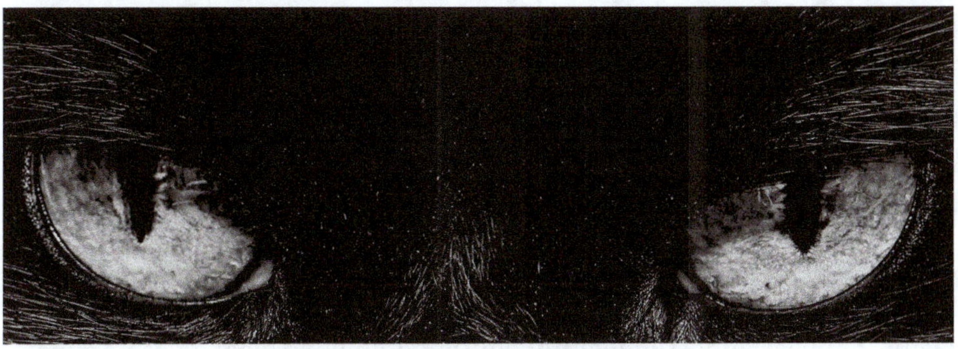

Figure 23: Not of this World (© Shutterstock)

EXTRATERRESTRIAL

The most credible image portrayed in various Sci-Fi entertainment media depicting an alien is that of a humanoid being with an enlarged head, a sleek, thin, hairless body and spindly limbs, who communicates with its pronounced large black eyes.

Figure 24 Fictional Alien (© Shutterstock)

The common feature of so many reported sightings (although rarely verified) is that of small spindly beings barely 1.5 metres in height, with extra-long arms, thin legs and an oversized head on a skinny neck. Facial features appear almost indeterminate (large bulbous black eyes dominate, with a tiny nose, indistinctive ears and a minuscule mouth).

Figure 25: Grey Alien (© Shutterstock)

Yet a single extraordinary close encounter with an almost human-like creature in July 1947 provided just such a credible verification.

American military officer Marion M. Magruder had been an ace fighter pilot and squadron leader in World War II. His prowess in successfully developing radar intercept night-fighting techniques for naval wartime pilots of single-engine aircraft in the Pacific ensured his long military career after the war.

The father of three was a Lieutenant Colonel when he eventually came face-to-face with the sole survivor of an alien UFO crash that occurred near Roswell in New Mexico. His remarkably accurate description of this being at close range provides a chilling insight into a live extraterrestrial.[3]

Its most compelling feature was its similarity to a human, '… the being had a flesh tone (pinkish skin)…although clearly, it was not from this planet'. The extraterrestrial was five feet tall or smaller, and appeared more like a child than a small adult, although its (disproportionately) large head and long arms meant it was not like a child. The head was not overlarge but its face '…had large eyes – larger than usual – and it had only a slit for a mouth and hardly any nose[4]… and no ears that he could discern'.[5]

'The strangest thing about its appearance … was the way it moved its long, spaghetti-like arms as if in a wavy motion. It looked "squiggly" …'[6]

****

In various respected scientific circles, there is a postulate that aliens are already on Earth. They may be here in the form of dormant microscopic organisms – potentially delivered as naturally embedded microbes in meteorites, trapped in cosmic debris from comets or as interstellar dust pervading our atmosphere, or transmitted as spores on radiation pressure waves from other stars – possibly since the times of earliest origins of the universe.

'Even today, about 100 tonnes of debris from comets and meteorites arrives on Earth daily.'[7] This debris is the most likely sources for such alien microbes.

Meteorites ejected from a parent planet afford encased biological materials adequate protection from space and solar radiation exposure during their interplanetary journey or during entry through Earth's atmosphere. Similarly, microbes trapped in cosmic dust particles escape super-heating processes by the gentle deceleration of the dust through the upper atmosphere.[8]

These are micro-organisms that are possibly able to initiate life upon finally reaching a suitably hospitable planetary environment. Certain bacteria have survived for prolonged periods travelling through space, despite experiencing interstellar extremes of radiation, temperature and pressure.

We call such resistant organisms *extremophiles*. They are highly resilient to environmental extremes that would be detrimental to most organisms found on Earth. It has merit in that even on our planet, most life is microscopic and subject to survival in environmental conditions that *Homo sapiens* would consider as relatively 'alien'.

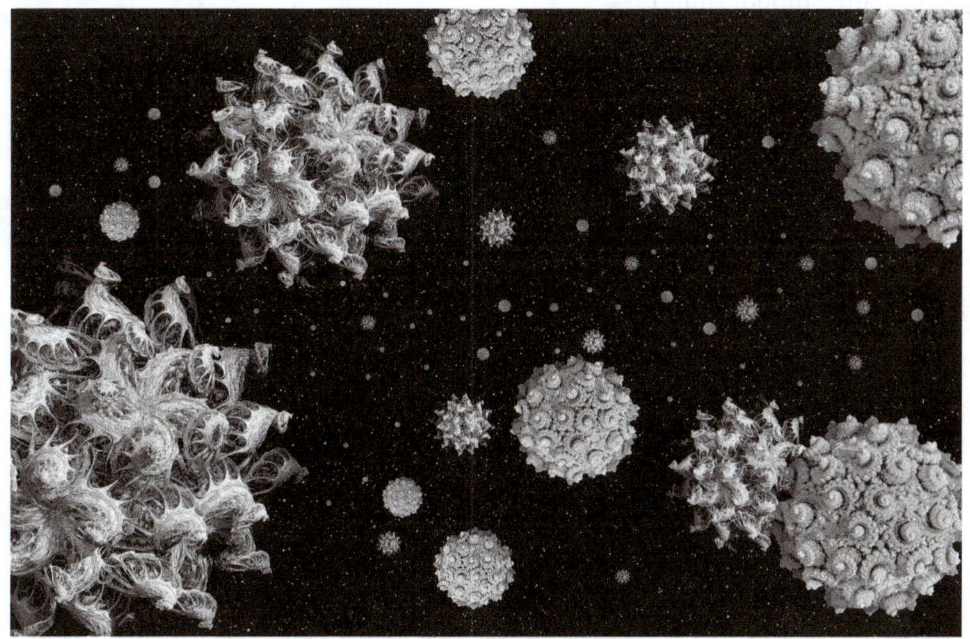

Figure 26: Spreading of Alien Seeds (© Shutterstock)

The question remains whether these complex microbial life-forms arrived by natural processes from space, or were intentionally directed here by advanced extraterrestrial intelligence. Do they indicate the presence of 'life' elsewhere in the universe?

For those scientists convinced these living organisms arrived by undirected means as an indirect basis for 'seeding of Earth with life' in conjunction with local evolutionary processes, two significant factors are of relevance.

The first is that this source is one feasible explanation for the absence of a myriad of hereditary transitional links (known as 'missing links') in the plant and animal kingdoms – the sudden appearance of new life-forms on Earth without any direct connection to immediate predecessors.[9] These may include introduced alien viruses that alter the evolutionary processes.

The second factor is that all micro-organisms, including extremophiles, have their genetic blueprint encoded by DNA, just the same as humans (and plants and animals).[10]

Evidence of fossilised extraterrestrial bacteria found in interstellar or inter-planetary matter transported to Earth was first discovered in the mid-1990s, and continues to be discovered. Most of the documented discoveries were the work of NASA.[11]

If this external introduction of dormant interstellar biological entities (DNA strands, living cells or bacteria) continues today, it may well remain as an integral evolutionary perhaps viral element to human development, partic-ularly when ancient bacterial spores 250 million years old are still able to be revived in the present.[12]

ALIEN INNOVATION

'Sorry, but your parts are worth a mint.' She drew her gun on the android. 'Every snowflake is special, until you need to make a snowball.'

T.R.Darling, *Quiet Pine Trees (2015)*

The main scientific focus on perceived extraterrestrial activity around the world has traditionally been confirming or disproving the existence of their spacecraft. It is these alien craft that transport such life-forms to our world, and consequently present the best available opportunity for us to observe, speculate and ideally confirm their technological capability.

However, without evident physical examination possible of such vessels beyond the highly sensitive and classified sources of military or select government agencies, such investigation is relatively limited to supposition and observations based upon vast anecdotal evidence and verified eyewitness accounts.

Probably the most pertinent technology to discuss is the mode of propulsion of these exotic and extremely sophisticated spacecraft. There have been several diverse theories proposed in the past, which have occasionally been scientifically justified.

EXTRATERRESTRIAL

These range from nuclear propulsion and ion drives, dark energy sources, anti-gravity systems and even biological organisms, to temporal (time) distortion devices and interdimensional transfer.

These are advanced technological systems that could plausibly transpose aliens across our galaxy, our universe and even time literally in the blink of an eye. If it sounds more like fantasy than factual, it is because the distinction between science fiction (what is possible but unlikely) and scientific fact (what is probable and realistic) can often be blurred.

All propulsion systems require some type of energy. We need to ask how it is generated, stored and converted to power the spacecraft across vast distances. The craft may be capable of traversing the boundaries of time itself.

Nuclear power derived from a tiny onboard reactor small enough to be housed in a spacecraft and delivering ion drive propulsion is probably not so remote from Earth's current advanced technological developments in particle accelerators of the 21st century.

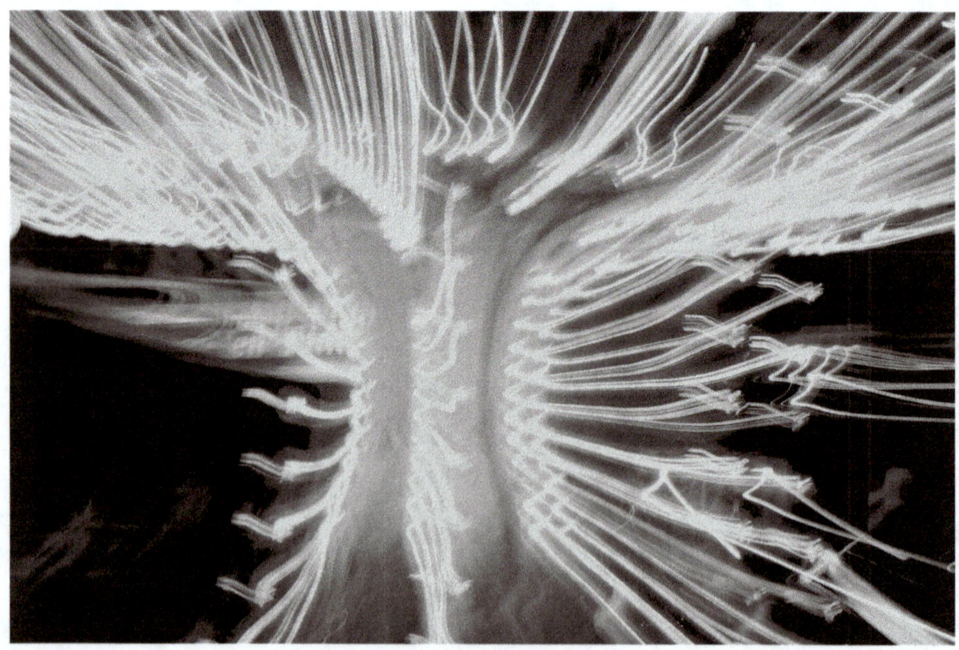

Figure 27: Supreme Propulsion Power (© Shutterstock)

Ion propulsion permits a slow but steady increase in speed until high velocity approaching light speed is reached, enabling the craft to maintain it for extended periods.

Temporal distortion, on the other hand, is an entirely new concept and requires due clarification.

Imagine a newly discovered, heavy radioactive chemical element that does not exist in nature and has been artificially synthesised. Then bombard this element with sufficient protons (subatomic particles with positive electric charge) causing it to decay and release immense energy.

It is this energy release in a spaceship which then '… draws space and time around the craft …the craft is pulled through space and time traversing incredible distances [in a slipstream] … Time stands still for those onboard, arriving at a destination at the moment of departure.'[1] Such enormous propulsion power creates its own temporal envelop around the spaceship.

Anti-gravity envelopes, which unify the effect of Earth's gravity and electromagnetism developed around spaceships, is another theoretical concept.

They would partially explain how such mysterious craft seem '… to hover in midair or move so slowly that conventional aircraft would stall at those speeds'.[2] With such an anti-gravity slipstream it may even be possible to increase vessel speed when accelerating in space to almost 60 per cent of light-speed.

Propulsion by living organism, such as the craft itself or through biological symbionts in contact with the spaceship pilot(s) appears an extreme concept. It has been suggested by some UFO witnesses. This system requires a direct biological interface between the alien or robotic pilot(s) and the living organism which provides the propulsion to drive the craft.

If biological engineering of spacecraft seems almost too fantastic, perhaps the following quotation from the 1984 Sci-Fi comedy movie *Repo Man* may provide further insight: 'There ain't no difference between a flying saucer and a time machine. People get so hung up on specifics. They miss out on seeing the whole thing.'[3]

Figure 28: Biological Propulsion (© Shutterstock)

Perhaps the most incredible form of alien propulsion is also the hardest to scientifically confirm at present.

This concept remains in the realms of the hypothetical: a self-sufficient propulsion system that draws on the infinite 'dark energy' of the universe itself, known as vacuum energy or ground state energy.

This potential source of unparalleled energy appears to be generated in the creation of virtual particles fluctuating in and out of existence in the vacuum of space. A scientific development to create propulsion using particles pushing off a vacuum known as the Quantum Vacuum Plasma Thruster has already been successfully tested by NASA in 2017.[4]

Interdimensional visits from other dimensions that co-exist separately from our dimension may not possibly even involve an alien spacecraft or propulsion process, but rather special 'devices' that travel between realities.[5]   Such means could possibly explain how such unidentified devices suddenly appear in the sky or the astronomical speed at which they readily dematerialise from sight or disappear from radar whilst departing our dimension.

****

   'Life is complicated. There are about 9 million known species on Earth, but vastly more unknown species; each a highly complex product of more than 3 billion years of evolution.'[6]

Now assume that on many other worlds elsewhere across our galaxy a similar evolutionary process is underway, except significantly more advanced than here on Earth. Life on such worlds may have been around for quite some time and the inhabitants may have accomplished sophisticated celestial space travel.

What technologies would they bring to our world if they appeared? How would we learn about such supremely advanced technology? Most importantly, how would we get access to their alien innovation?

Some possible technological examples cited in various literature as being 'of extraterrestrial origin' include a (spacesuit) fabric that was indestructible and remarkably tensile, ultra-thin metal that could not be permanently deformed or damaged and always returned to original shape, flat round computer circuits not yet invented or developed, and a cutting tool akin to a laser weapon.

If it sounds too fanciful to be correct, then think again. Many modern technological developments throughout the world really only began to gain traction from about midway through the 20th century.

Consider remarkable and innovative technological inventions, such as computers, micro-chip circuitry, robotics, jet engines, space travel, permanent satellites, radio astronomy, stealth bombers and drone aircraft, lasers, ground-breaking advances in medical research and worldwide telecommunications... These have arrived in a relatively brief time period – over the past 70 years.

EXTRATERRESTRIAL

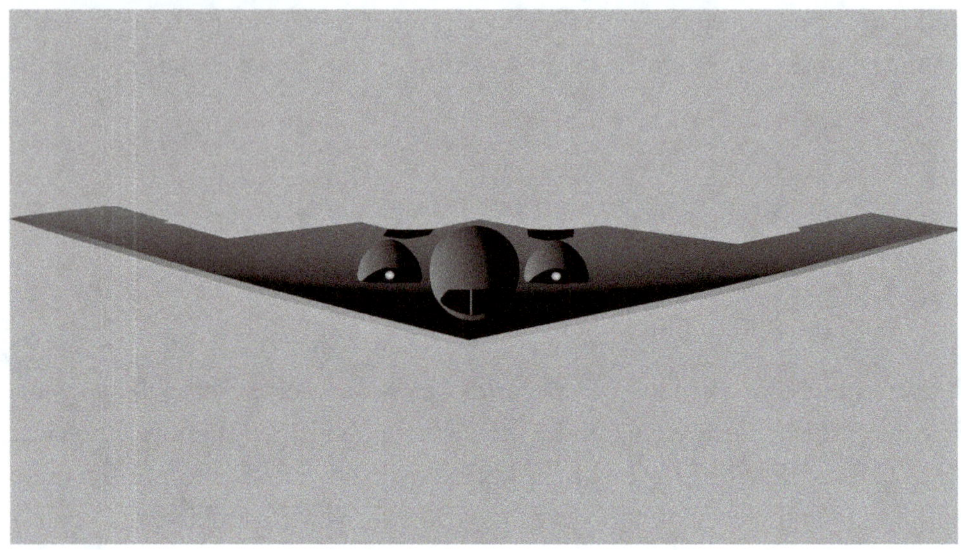

Figure 29: Stealth Aircraft (© Shutterstock)

Homo sapiens of the present 21st century now enjoy technology that was only previously found in science fiction magazines and comics in the 1950s.

Have any of these human advancements been assisted by the arrival of extraterrestrial technologies? One suggested source has been by retrieval from an alien spacecraft that crashed in July 1947 in New Mexico, USA.

****

Unexpected arrivals of alien spacecraft may also provide other rare glimpses into their inherent technologies. The Rendlesham Forest UFO that landed in the aforementioned forest in Suffolk, England in late 1980 is possibly the most famous of such events to occur in the United Kingdom, probably due to the immense volume of credible detail reported about the incident by those involved.

One eyewitness to this landing, in the early hours of 26th December, was US Air Force Staff Sergeant James (Jim) Penniston who got close enough to touch the side of this 'craft of unknown origin'. The craft's hull had strange pictorial markings which he likened to 'ancient Egyptian hieroglyphs', and subsequently sketched in his USAF-issued notebook. These diagrammatic symbols of inscriptions would prove to be invaluable in supporting what he experienced during that encounter. To the unaccustomed, such alien symbols would seem relatively meaningless, but to an experienced person skilled in USAF security such as Sergeant Penniston, this was important detail.[7]

The markings were a series of small symbols about three to four inches (7.5 -10cms) in height and covering a diameter of about three feet (0.9m) on the left hand exterior side of the craft. The raised symbols were etched onto the craft's smooth seamless exterior surface.[8] Sergeant Penniston recalled touching the strange markings with his hand.[9]

The pictorial glyph-like markings included three singular odd shapes and two segmented shapes In addition, there was also a separate circle enclosing a triangle with 'same size circular objects'; a small solid black circle set at its tip and another solid black circle at the bottom right-hand apex. This triangle was the largest symbol and centred in the middle of the others.[10]

A diagrammatic sketched representation by Jim Penniston of these symbols from his notebook can be found on page 7 of *Encounter in Rendlesham Forest: The Inside Story of the World's Best-Documented UFO Incident* by Nick Pope and first published in 2014.

To some, such unusual shapes and symbols might suggest military markings, perhaps used on a highly secretive and experimental prototype or drone aircraft. This was not to be the case.

Whatever the pictorial symbols represented, touching them appeared to have quite an influence on this eyewitness. In 2010, James Penniston subsequently revealed that on the following day after touching the pictorial glyphs, he was able to produce 16 pages of binary code (number ones and zeros) in a notebook. 'The binary codes, were a direct result of contact with a physical craft. A craft of unknown origin. Meaning it was a unidentified craft and where it came from is still unknown'.[11]

Of the many meanings decoded from this array of binary coding, a few words truly stand-out to me about the possible intent of this craft of unknown origin: 'Exploration of Humanity'.[12]

EXTRATERRESTRIAL

On a previous occasion, about 180 years ago, another mysterious craft arrived with text written in an unknown language; this time decorating the inner side of this spherical 'capsule-like' object.

This encounter has become an integral part of Japanese folklore, a myth and a legend. It apparently arose in 1803 when a USO (unidentified submerged object) was found drifting in waters on the eastern coast of Japan.

This object was known as Utsuro-bune ('hollow ship') and its strange symbols may have been an older version of our alphabet, with the following exception that it shared in common with the Rendlesham Forest UFO: the

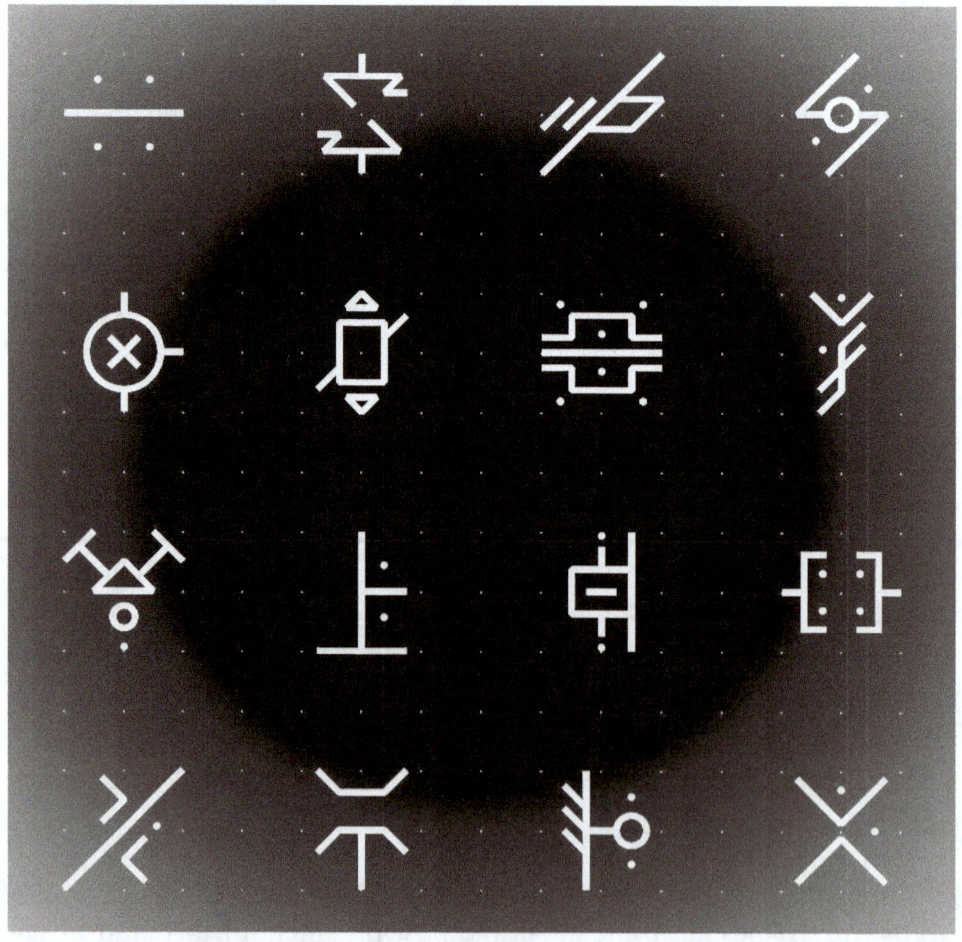

Figure 30: Various Identifier Symbols (© Shutterstock)

placement of circles.

The Utsuro-bune had pictorial symbols indicating two small circles located on opposing sides of a triangle, and one small circle located on a single side of another triangle. The Rendlesham UFO had the smaller circles at the triangle apexes.[13] The significance of these strange 'alien' symbols possibly shared between two different unknown craft remains unresolved.

From time to time, people who have reported seeing unidentified flying craft have also noticed strange 'alien" markings on such objects, often distinguishable due to the unusual nature of the distinctive symbols displayed. These sightings are uncommon and any exterior hull markings are not usually able to be physically touched by an eyewitness.

Deciphering such hieroglyphic symbols presents further issues, particularly where such craft of alien origin may be despatched from entirely different sectors of the universe.

Whatever figurative shapes and symbols may be represented on these spacecraft, they are not of our world.

ARE WE ALONE?

A still more glorious dawn awaits
Not a sunrise, but a galaxy rise
A morning filled with 400 billion suns
The rising of the milky way.

Carl Sagan, *Cosmos (1980)*

Consider that the Milky Way Galaxy in which our planet is located comprises a minimum estimated number of 100 billion stars, without including any other galaxies or clusters of galaxies located throughout the universe. Assume that only a miniscule one percent of these star systems contain a single habitable planet, and this still represents one billion worlds that potentially harbour alien life.

The greatest drawback to extending our knowledge of such planets is the astronomical distances between our world and these stars.

Interstellar travel at hyperlight speed permitting passage exceeding the speed of light is not within our present knowledge of space technology. Exploratory voyages in the present would be measured in hundreds of Earth years rather than in months, involving multiple human generations to satisfactorily complete each journey.

This is not necessarily the case for more advanced civilisations that may exist elsewhere in the cosmos.

It has been suggested that intelligent life and civilisations could have begun to appear in our galaxy at least five billion years ago (the minimum estimated time for any intelligent life to arise on an Earth-like world). If this is the case, such alien life existed some time before the creation of our own solar system.[1]

Astrophysicist and author Jeffrey Bennett provides useful and salient guidance on this dilemma by proffering three possible solutions. The first and least credible is that we are actually alone due to an absence or extreme rarity of any galactic civilisation.

The second is that galactic civilisation is common elsewhere, but colonisation of our galaxy has not occurred, either due to lack of satisfactory technology or failure of would-be colonists to survive the exploration process. This only applies to our sector of the galaxy, yet still represents a plausible but ominous outcome for our future exploits.[2]

The third and most credible solution is that there is a galactic civilisation and '… it has existed for millions or billions of years before us …but that we are not yet capable of discovering its existence'. Furthermore, such alien civilisations are either deliberately concealing themselves and so not interfering in our emerging civilisation or '… have no reason to bother with us on our planet'.[3]

The most likely outcome: 'If we successfully navigate the adolescence of our civilization, there's a universe full of grownups awaiting our arrival.'[4]

Seeking and confirming Earth-like similar planets elsewhere in our galaxy would probably be a tremendous starting point to detect new life-forms, given the abundant and complex life systems present on our world.

Such extrasolar planets (outside our solar system) or exoplanets as they were subsequently named, have been identified since the 1990's, and now total 3,823 confirmed planets in 2,860 systems as of 29th August 2018.[5]

EXTRATERRESTRIAL

Figure 31: Search for Exoplanets (© Shutterstock)

Earth-*sized* planets that exist in a 'circumstellar habitable zone' (i.e. the range of orbits around a star within which a planetary surface is able to support liquid water given sufficient atmospheric pressure[6]) may yet be instrumental in identifying Earth-*like* extraterrestrial life. The criteria for habitability has since expanded to incorporate various other potential factors required for the creation and sustenance of life.

The problem with successfully identifying life on any of these Earth-like exoplanets is that, of the select few that appear the most promising, there are still arduous and inhospitable environments to overcome.

These include the unpredictable activity of each sun-like star, which can be entirely different to our Sun, and the predicted size and surface temperatures of the planets, which may be somewhat extreme, affecting the potential for suitable habitability of alien life.

An additional complication is whether such planets can actually support carbon-based life such as ourselves, or even possible silicone- or ammonia-based alien life-forms.

The most recent encouraging sign of such habitable exoplanets has been the 2016 discovery of the Trappist-1 single star system of seven Earth-size planets, of which three are located firmly in the habitable zone.

This batch of exoplanets is relatively close to Earth – 40 light years (378 trillion kilometres) away – and closely orbits an ultra-cool red dwarf sun that could permit the potential for liquid water. The planets are also very close to each other and all mostly made of rock, but contain up to 5 percent of water.

They may also be tidally locked to their dwarf star, resulting in the same side of each planet always facing this star, and either in perpetual day or night, with weather patterns including extreme temperatures totally unlike Earth.[7]

In February 2018, additional density measurements refined the planetary investigation of the entire system. Exoplanet Trappist -1e; the middle planet of the system was the only one in the system that appeared to be slightly denser than Earth, suggesting a large iron core. Its size, density and amount of radiation received from its star make this exoplanet the most similar to our home planet.[8]

Figure 32: Trappist-1 Exoplanets (© Shutterstock)

EXTRATERRESTRIAL

The refinement of these bulk densities has determined that the hotter planets closer to the parent dwarf star are likely to host water as atmospheric vapour and those more distant probably as ice frozen on their surfaces. However, the presence of water on exoplanet Trappist-1e (and 1c) is not necessarily a thick layer of atmospheric vapour, ocean or ice as evident on the remaining planets. It is indicative of a thin atmosphere (possibly even thinner than on Earth).[9]

> 'However, it remains to be seen whether the TRAPPIST-1 water is present on the surface of the exoplanet [the entire system] in vast, deep oceans, or whether it is as vapour in a dense, steamy atmosphere, or whether it is spread around in the exoplanet, much like how Earth's mantle contains the equivalent amount of water as in the oceans.'[10]

****

With a view to identifying any potential exoplanet reasonably close to Earth, scientists have been evaluating Alpha Centauri over many years. It is the nearest star system to our solar system and located in the southern

Figure 33: Target Exoplanet (© Shutterstock)

constellation Centaurus of the Milky Way. It consists of three stars, including a small and faint red dwarf named Proxima Centauri.

Orbiting this star is an exoplanet of similar mass to Earth and a mere 4.2 light years (40 trillion kilometres) away. The discovery of Proxima b (also called Proxima Centauri b or Alpha Centauri Cb) in the 'habitable zone' of its star was announced in August 2016.[11]

The dwarf star Proxima Centauri is smaller and 1,000 times weaker than our Sun, but the close orbit of Proxima b of only 7.5 million kilometres places this rocky terrestrial exoplanet at a suitable distance from its parent star for conditions to be potentially temperate and 'habitable' for life.[12]

A scientific research team including astrophysicists at the French National Center for Scientific Research (CNRS) in conjunction with Cornell University conducted computer simulations to ascertain the potential characteristics of this small rocky world. Their report was published in October 2016.

They determined that this planet may very well host liquid water on its surface, potentially with Earth-like water contents or as a single liquid ocean 200 km deep (where the planet is larger than expected), and possessing a thin, gassy atmosphere that could surround the planet, like on Earth, rendering such an exoplanet potentially life-friendly.[13]

If seeking to discover extraterrestrial intelligence on very distant planets, the preliminary stage would be to first identify a most important criterion for life – the molecular structure of the living organism.

For humans, animals and plants on our world, this requirement is carbon-based, that is '… long chains of carbon atoms attached to various other atoms such as hydrogen, oxygen and nitrogen'.[14]

Plants derive their carbon from the environment and in turn are consumed by animals, and people, who derive their carbon accordingly by similar consumption of both. What if aliens are not carbon-based beings?

Silica-based life has particular limitations: there is no easy way to extract silicon from the environment as it is traditionally found in solid forms; and it only forms exceptionally weak molecular bonds compared with carbon,

EXTRATERRESTRIAL

thus is a relatively fragile building block for life.

Despite its supreme abundance over carbon in the Earth's crust, *silicon* has not been the foundation for our life-forms. Of course, this does not exclude other mineral-based cellular structures as yet unknown to the human species.

Figure 34: Crystalline Silica (© Shutterstock)

The search for exotic living organisms on our world living in inhospitable or extreme biological conditions that may mimic life on other planets has yet to substantiate silica-based forms.

Scientists have identified that nature could probably successfully incorporate silicon into our carbon-based molecules (the basic components for life), which is a very useful indicator that life is flexible and adaptable.

It still does not confirm that discrete silicon- or organosilicon-based life is biologically possible.

Another advanced possibility raised by cosmologist and space scientist Martin Rees looks into our own perceived evolutionary future and ponders whether we will continue as organic beings who may find '… a way to avoid or indefinitely delay the natural processes of aging and death [attain immortality] …or no longer remain biological entities by becoming silicon-based.[15]

Such life-forms as contemporary artificially intelligent (AI) humanoids are silicon-based and are being developed at present to overcome our physical limitations.

If alien life elsewhere has already transcended from a biological form to a hybrid silicon being, we may need to be searching for a highly technological life force without any prerequisite for our suitable atmosphere and water in order to survive.

Figure 35: Hybrid (© Shutterstock)

The essential requirement for most if not all life on Earth is the presence of liquid water.

Yet what if alien life exists in conjunction with other liquids, such as ammonia for example? Nevertheless, as far as we know, water remains the superior medium to support and nurture life, and hence is a natural target in identifying suitable exoplanets.

INCURSIONS

'Almost every species in the universe has an irrational fear of the dark. But they're wrong. 'Cause it's not irrational … It's what's in the dark. It's what's always in the dark.'[1]

Tenth Doctor Who, *Silence in the Library (2008)*

Extraterrestrial incursions into our modern society by direct contact, personal communications and even interference in our daily lives is worth contemplating, if such beings actually exist.

However, rational explanations for their presence and intentions might be rather difficult to identify, primarily because sightings and encounters are often only based upon scant physical evidence and are thus difficult to verify.

Witnesses may be reluctant or too embarrassed to divulge these possible encounters for fear of ridicule, humiliation or condemnation. Encounters able to be verified by independent onlookers appear to be quite uncommon and when reported publicly, are usually subjected to both intense scientific scrutiny and assessment of personnel credibility.

Such unusual events will probably be dissected to determine their veracity, with dire outcomes for any likely witnesses. Perhaps 'the incursion'

EXTRATERRESTRIAL

is a product of a fanciful imagination, a surreal experience mistaken for something quite innocent, a deceptive hoax or prank, or some other ulterior motive. The onus will always rest on the witness to prove beyond a shadow of doubt that such an extraterrestrial encounter occurred, and thereby lies the dilemma.

The sceptical nature of *Homo sapiens* means they usually remain unconvinced and doubt the hearsay of others without concrete proof, especially when the story involves extraordinary or rare sightings of aliens, UFOs and any similar celestial oddities likely to arouse suspicion.

This dilemma has an added complexity, which is probably the most important factor of all: what if the supposed extraterrestrial life-form's intent is to remain concealed, undetectable and secretive as possible?

Figure 36: Watching and Waiting (© Shutterstock)

An example of a difficult-to-verify UFO encounter involves a preacher and his unfortunate sighting of a UFO that was to haunt his life for a considerable period of years thereafter.

Although not reporting the event to anyone else, the preacher became convinced that he was being followed and stalked by an unseen entity. He endured a series of bizarre events that resulted in considerable personal distress to him.

After ten years, he was visited by beings who freely demonstrated their ability to assume whatever form they chose, including changing shape, emitting light from their bodies (bioluminescence) and materialising/dematerialising at will.

The preacher was even permitted to photograph them, although to avoid public ridicule, only confided this bizarre experience to his family members and closest friends. Within days, he was visited by three 'policemen' keen to view his photographs of otherworldly entities. These officers wished to get the imagery published of such alien life to expose such creatures to the world.[2]

The same policemen returned the following evening and confiscated the photographs, before abducting the preacher and dumping him in a remote wooded area. The shapeshifters had returned disguised as bogus police-men, removed his photographs, and a few months later, the preacher developed afflictions, including temporary impaired vision and a scaly upper torso resulting from direct contact with them.[3]

There was no further intervention from these shapeshifters or paranormal entities thereafter. If these beings are able to assume whatever disguise so suits them, the incursion becomes most difficult to predict, as 'things are seldom what they seem in that world'.

****

Alien incursions do not necessarily require intentional personal contact with witnesses, as the events of the night of 12th September 1952 illustrated to some residents of the small American town of Flatwoods, West Virginia.

On this autumn evening, there had already been reports of 'strange lights and objects in the skies' prevalent across the country, so it was not totally unexpected that this region may also encounter such phenomena.

'Numerous people in a 20-mile radius saw illuminated objects in the sky at the same time.'[4]

The landing by a silvery saucer-like craft on one side of a nearby hilltop just on dark at about 7 pm and witnessed by a small group of town children was certainly unexpected.

Upon approaching the area, the children and a supervising adult observed 'a globular-shaped object emitting a reddish light pulsating from dim to bright at regular intervals'. It was not this strange craft that was particularly

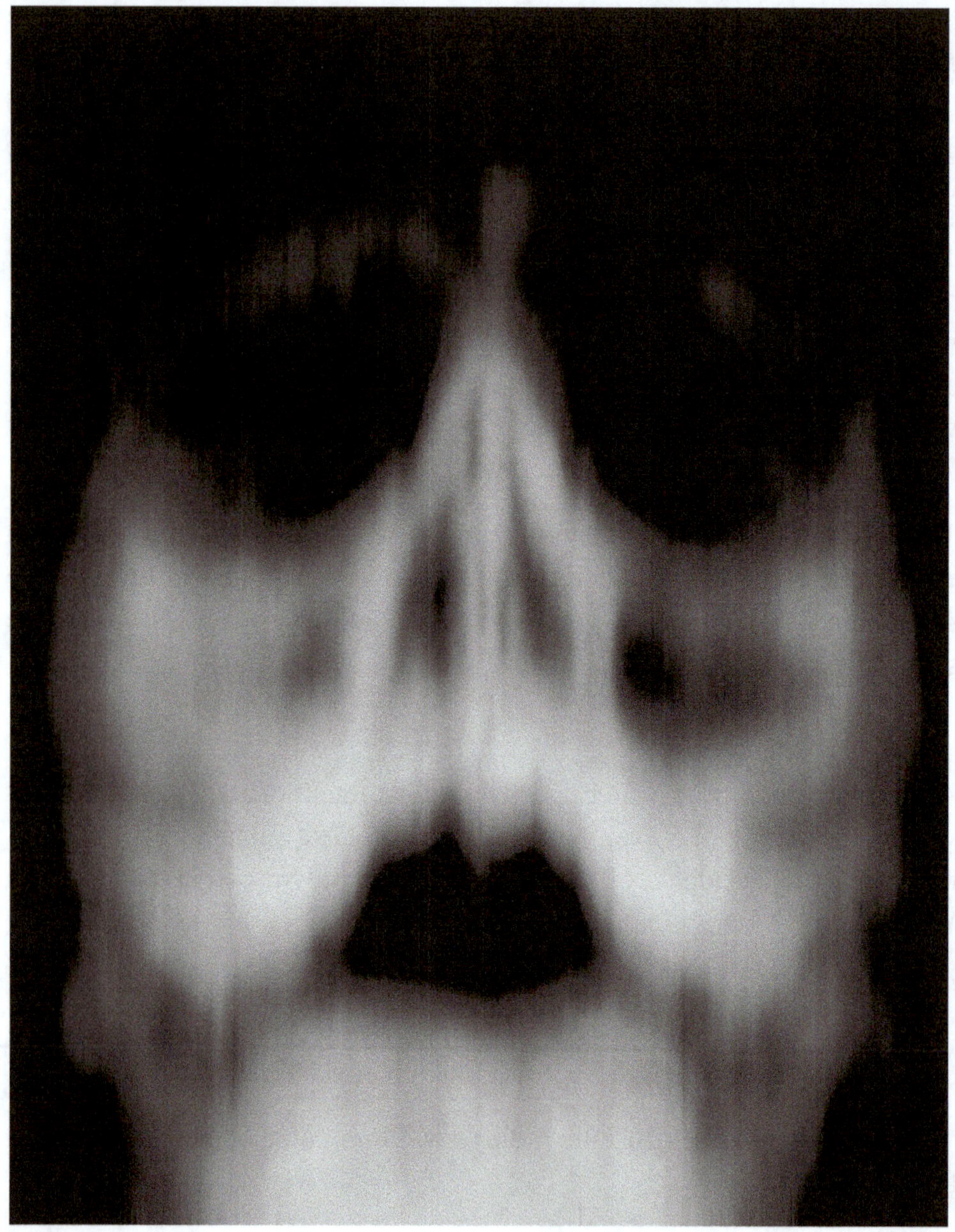

Figure 37: Shapeshifters (© Shutterstock)

terrifying, but the presence of a huge, towering man-like figure standing nearby.

Described as no more than three metres in height, the 'biped being' may

'…have been a robot … or some entity inside a suit that would adapt the wearer to Earth's atmosphere'.[5] The figure was moving toward the group but in a direction that would eventually lead down to the craft. Its movement was not by walking or jumping, but by moving evenly (a gliding motion).

A flashlight had been initially shone on the figure to gain a better view of its appearance, and this act may have stimulated the entity into moving towards its spacecraft. The frightened group fled without any further hesitation.

The other extraordinary feature of this encounter was the prevalence of a mist resembling fog but with a pungent, irritating odour that was sickening and foul. This mist became denser upon approaching the spacecraft and was described by some 'like burning metal or sulphur'.[6]

The only traces reportedly remaining when the site was re-visited later that evening was the residual smell of the foul odour at ground level and oil residue as an odd, gummy deposit. Some 'skid 'marks' were observed in the tall grass on the following morning between where the figure had been sighted and the craft.[7]

The purpose of the alien landing and subsequent incursion by the strange figure remain unresolved. It may have been either from necessity or to make observations, but whatever the purpose, the descriptions provided by several witnesses confirm they did see *something* that night.

UFO sightings extracted from Project Blue Book around this date provide some interesting commentary.

At 9:30 pm that same evening in Allen, Maryland and located only 400 kilometres east of Flatwoods, a UFO was observed flying north-east. This was two and one half hours after the Flatwoods incursion. Two members of the U.S. Ground Observer Corps (an auxiliary of the USAF Air Defense Command) tracked the unknown object by binoculars for a duration of 35 minutes. The object was described as a white light with red trim and streamers [possibly the trailing glow] (Case No. 2077).

EXTRATERRESTRIAL

> *In the early evening of the following day 13 September, a light aircraft pilot reported a UFO overhead near Allentown, Pennsylvania about 430 kilometres north-east of Flatwoods,. The object was described as 3 foot (1 metre) and shaped like a fat football flaming orange-red color that briefly manoeuvred around his aircraft before disappearing (Case No. 2085).*

****

Incursions may also have a more surreptitious intent, such as the reported claims worldwide of human abductions by extraterrestrial entities. Some of these have been intensively investigated and scientifically analysed. Some select prominent examples include the most famous case of Betty and Barney Hill (1961, USA), Travis Walton (1976, USA) and Alan Godfrey (1980, UK).

In mid-1980, Constable Alan Godfrey had been investigating the mysterious death of a coalminer who had disappeared five days earlier and whose corpse had been discovered outdoors on top of a coal heap in West Yorkshire. The body appeared to have been undressed and redressed entirely but incorrectly, and was missing certain clothing and all personal effects.

There were also no '…residual footprints, tire tracks, or tread marks' indicating how the body reached the top of the 3.6 metre high coal tip. Furthermore, the corpse was clean of any coal dust and had a distinguishable pattern of precise burn marks around the base of the skull that had an unidentifiable ointment (green-yellow gel) applied.[8]

Some six months later and still in the local area, the constable was investigating a case of missing cattle who were to be eventually located in a different location, but without any identifiable tracks indicating how they reached this field.

The herd was in a park nearby to the road, where the constable was to have quite an encounter. The constable was driving along this road just after 5 am when he encountered '… a diamond-shaped object, very bright, hovering just above the road surface and spinning very rapidly'.[9] This flying object was estimated to be about 20 feet (6 metres) high and 14 feet (4.3

Figure 38: Where Are We? (© Shutterstock)

metres) wide and hovering in the middle of the road.[10]

There were subsequent reports from other credible witnesses confirming the silent, bright unidentified light, but for Constable Godfrey, the encounter was far more concerning. During his brief encounter with the flying object, an estimated a period of 15 minutes went unaccounted from his memory.

Under subsequent regression hypnosis, the constable recalled being inside the flying craft and meeting '… one humanoid alien and robot-like small creatures with large heads…'It also appeared that the exterior of the constable's boot '… had been damaged (split) as if being dragged along a hard surface'.[11]

Regrettably, the constable's recollections remained unclear about what eventuated whilst inside the craft.

The remarkable and unusual circumstances that presented to Alan Godfrey in his investigations and the missing segment of his memory remain unresolved today, but do provide intriguing insight into the potential presence of unidentified external forces at work.

****

Various causes have been attributable to such claims about human abductions by aliens.

These include elaborate hoaxes, mistaken, delusional or fanciful interpretations of events arising from sleep deprivation, stress or dreams, suspicious disappearances and contrived criminal cover-ups. Some have suggested secretive military involvement due to the highly sensitive nature of possible alien arrivals.

The dilemma for investigators is that abduction witnesses usually have little physical tangible evidence to support the event, relying instead upon a verbal version of events that in some cases must be obtained by hypnosis.

In many verified cases abductees have experienced memory loss for a period of unaccounted time. Some cases involved possibly inexplicable changes to the abductees and to select associated objects or apparel, and under stringent scientific hypnosis, abductees recalled encounters with otherworldly beings of various descriptions.

In the extensively investigated case of Betty and Brian Hill, the purpose of the brief abduction was eventually identified under hypnotic regression as a detailed anatomical examination of their bodies.

Periods of unaccounted time appear to be common in so many cases, as is the detailed descriptions of these extraterrestrial visitors. They have variously been described as short or tall humanoids, strange bipedal reptilians and large insect-like beings, or even shadowy ethereal 'energy' figures. Is this simply the product of a vivid imagination at work or the reality of an actual incursion?

Figure 39: Incursion (© Shutterstock)

****

An overview of intentional alien incursions reveals they tend to be either for surveillance/observation purposes of our world, or for the physical collection of specimens, including plants, soils, minerals, water, as well as wild and domesticated animals.

Preferred surveillance may encompass strategic structures (defence installations, power generation plants, dams) and observations involve personnel, preferably selecting individuals or small groups for further examination onboard. These activities are typically conducted on dusk or early evening to reduce the likely risk of detection.

If interrupted, the spacecraft may sometimes return at a more suitable time.

EXTRATERRESTRIAL

Such vessels may also employ their onboard weaponry in moderation, including various heat or force beams. These tools can be effectively applied to immobilise vehicles and people.[12]

Where the incursion is unplanned due to spacecraft malfunction or damage, the occupants usually avoid human contact and depart as soon as expedient. Extraterrestrials do not appear to seek open communication with us, suggesting their incursions are relatively furtive.

UNIVERSAL BIOSIGNATURES

The best proof that there's intelligent life in outer space is the fact that it hasn't come here...the fact that we have not yet found the slightest evidence for life — much less intelligence — beyond this Earth does not surprise or disappoint me in the least.

Arthur C. Clarke, *British Science and Sci-Fi Writer*

Perhaps the ultimate conundrum for astronomers seeking definitive answers to the ageless question about alien life elsewhere in the universe are the choices available.

Assume that there is intelligent extraterrestrial life and that it exists on distant 'habitable' planets yet to be detected by our high resolution telescopes or interplanetary probes.

Now further assume such planets have or had suitable biological chemistry and atmosphere conducive to form life *as we know it* – living organisms that thrive on the same essential molecules and satisfactory environmental conditions that created and currently preserve our vast empire of life on Earth.

Unfortunately, any hypothesis about such matters delves into murky waters. Earth relies upon the presence of water as probably the main contributor to sustain our life-forms. This liquid is crucial to the health of most complex organic molecules. Our world relies upon the process of living plant photosynthesis absorbed from sunlight to regenerate a clean habitable atmosphere by introducing oxygen into the air as a natural by-product. The planet is located at just the right distance from the Sun to comfortably sustain life.

Yet are we right to assume that intelligent alien life requires such essentials simply because they have worked so well for us?

Figure 40: Alternative World (© Shutterstock)

Are these conditions or similar variations mandatory for life throughout the universe? Is Earth merely one evolutionary example not necessarily reproduced anywhere else?

The evolutionary processes of planets and of their life species can be complex and relatively unique in duration and outcomes. It would be most unlikely in our universe that two planets have evolved identically, particularly if the essential life resource of water is not present on both.

To further complicate the matter, consider what it must involve for the native intelligent species to evolve to such a sophisticated level that it is able to undertake interstellar travel.

Now assume that our comprehension of intelligent life *based upon Earth's biosignature* is not replicated elsewhere in the universe, and that our planet is home to unique species based upon specific evolutionary processes. Time to alter our vision of what equates to life elsewhere in the cosmos.

There are a couple of avenues available to scientists seeking alternatives to locate and identify such intelligent alien life. The first choice seems the most expedient but probably offers the lower percentage for success, and that is to intercept their radio transmission messages.

It is a noisy universe with much happening on the airwaves emitted by innumerable natural sources:

'Outside the solar system, the sources of radio waves includes clouds of gas and dust, stars of various kinds such as pulsars (rapidly rotating neutron stars), quasers (short for 'quasi-stellar radio sources', galaxies during early stages of their life), black holes … and galaxies (usually elliptical galaxies).[1]

Within our solar system, the Sun is our most intense natural source of radio waves, and this compounds the difficulty of receiving any potential artificially transmitted signals from the cosmos clearly. This 'symphony of distinctive noise' can be highly variable or repetitive at various times, and anything in between at other times.

If we are seeking to intercept alien radio wave transmissions amongst this cacophony of sound, it might prove rather difficult unless the signals are directed specifically to us, and in a form that is readily decipherable.

The likelihood of potential neighbours actively instigating contact with us remains slim. Advanced extraterrestrials capable of transmissions across the universe or from interplanetary craft may also theoretically be expecting a reply.

The second choice for scientists is to accept that intelligent extraterrestrial

EXTRATERRESTRIAL

life does not resemble anything we could anticipate due to the immense biometric variables involved.

Radically different life-forms could possibly evolve based upon the vast complexity of the universe – not the least being the myriad of star systems in the skies. Many evolutionary factors are required to form and sustain life, and it could be expected such 'evolutionary branches' that created intelligent humans would be most unlikely to be reproduced.

Figure 41: Alien Landscape (© Shutterstock)

'You can find self-replicating vortexes in the atmosphere of the Sun. There are all sorts of self-reproducing systems in all sorts of environments which could hold potential for life.'[2]

Are we likely to be in for some surprises at first contact, and when will there be verifiable contact?

This is where a suitable definition of life that is both scientific and practical becomes fuzzy, as all we have is an Earth-based template for the existence of life-forms.

Speculative evaluation of potential alien life rests upon future space exploration and detailed detection of suitable exoplanets that may harbour such life. There is little doubt that whatever we discover in the process will be particularly challenging and yet enlightening.

****

For those contemplating what such new worlds may resemble, consider the following story from the American television science fiction series *The Twilight Zone* hosted by Rod Serling between 1959 and 1964.

In the episode entitled 'Probe 7, Over and Out' and aired on CBS (Columbia Broadcast System) in the last season of the series, the planet selected by this particular astronaut was not by choice. It was a small, remote planet deep in space and several million miles away from the home world of the solitary astronaut who had just crash-landed there.

Although surviving the landing, the astronaut was badly injured and his spaceship seemingly beyond repair. He had been set adrift in an ocean of space in a metal lifeboat that had been scorched and destroyed and would never fly again.

Fortunately, he was still able to contact his base requesting rescue, but was informed that his home planet was on the verge of war and no spacecraft could be despatched. Whilst the marooned traveller explored the surroundings, the last transmission received from home base had a dire warning. Radiation from the ensuing war had made his world uninhabitable and eventually would kill any remaining survivors.

There was to be no rescue mission. However, this small planet did have similar gravity and an atmosphere to his world, offering him a second chance at life, albeit a lonely life. It was then that the astronaut realised he was not alone.

A human-like female had also become stranded as the only survivor of her doomed planet. Although not sharing the same language, the couple soon communicated using various gestures and signs. Her name was Eve

EXTRATERRESTRIAL

Norda and his name Adam Cook, and the female called this strange planet 'Earth'. They chanced upon a fertile garden-like area in which native fruit grew abundantly – an idyllic paradise for starting a new life, similar to the biblical 'garden of Eden'; Adam and Eve in a new beginning.[3]

Figure 42: Garden of Paradise (© Shutterstock)

The narrator of this episode aptly concluded: 'Do you know these people? Names familiar, are they? They lived a long time ago. Perhaps they're part fable, perhaps they're part fantasy. And perhaps the place they're walking to now is not really called 'Eden'.'[4]

OUR ASTRAL DESTINY

That's one small step for [a] man, one giant leap for mankind.

Neil Armstrong, *Apollo 11 Moon Landing (1969)*

If humans are ultimately destined to become successful interstellar explorers and colonists across the cosmos, we must expect a protracted evolutionary period. Modern humans (the subspecies *Homo sapiens sapiens*) only commenced colonising the world an estimated 125,000 – 60,000 years ago.

We live on a planet that formed around 4.6 billion years ago located in a solar system about 5 billion years of age. By such comparisons, it becomes most evident that our species has not been around long, and has quite a significant journey of development ahead to evolve into proficient space (and time) travellers who can safely endure celestial expeditions.

Our solar system is within the Milky Way Galaxy that has been estimated to have formed almost 14 billion years ago. Given the age of these planetary systems, it would seem almost inevitable that there should be other intelligent species more advanced than us somewhere on those myriad of alien worlds.

The extreme diversity of physical shapes and flight characteristics of in-

EXTRATERRESTRIAL

explicable flying objects observed throughout our history is extraordinary, therefore it is most likely that we are being visited by spacecraft from various alien cultures.

These aliens are almost certainly life-forms that have not only been existence far longer than humans, but who have developed advanced technologies superior to those of our world.

We are talking about extraterrestrial life that can easily transit both space and time to venture far and wide, and it may be closer than you might imagine.

Figure 43: Great Expectations (© depositphotos)

The space flight missions of the Apollo program (Project Apollo) conducted by NASA from 1966 to 1972 eventually culminated in several manned lunar landings by astronauts, commencing with Apollo 11 on 20th July 1969. Such flights around the Moon and carefully co-ordinated landings provided the world with incredibly detailed imagery of our only natural satellite. The missions also obtained samples of geological material of a planet other than Earth.

Highly skilled and intensively trained astronauts were employed to ensure the various elaborate equipment despatched on each mission was correctly installed and operated to gather considerable data about the Moon's environment.

Occasionally there would be reported observations of peculiar or odd objects in space above the planet or on the Moon's surface.

Tangible explanations were provided by NASA for such astronaut sightings, such as disused componentry of spacecraft jettisoned into space during the flight(s), anomalies arising in the high-tech imagery reproduction, faulty equipment or other operational causes.

There were instances when the odd events reported by the astronauts' appeared to be inexplicable. For example, there was a two-minute interruption to sound and image transmission between the astronauts and NASA's Mission Control in Houston during the first lunar landing.

The official NASA public response for the unusual transmission silence was the overheating malfunction of one of the two television cameras on the mission, thereby disrupting output.

This was an interesting development for Apollo 11, given the operational status of both cameras and the quality resolution of their images were of critical importance to the success of the project, with camera function issues reviewed more than any other technical component throughout the mission.[1]

It was claimed by unnamed amateur ham radio operators on Earth who had been receiving VHF signals on their own facilities that they had intercepted radio signals from astronaut Neil Armstrong on the moon during the mission,[2] and this included the same two minute malfunction period.

A subsequently published account of this specific intercept appears to have been widely dismissed by the world's media. Separate excerpts of this intercepted transmission that reportedly took place between the two astronauts and Mission Control are provided:

> *Apollo 11 (calling Mission Control): 'These babies are huge, sir ... enormous....Oh, God, you wouldn't believe it! I'm telling you there are other space craft out there... lined up on the far side of the crater edge... they're on the moon watching us ...' Saga's UFO Special Magazine, Vol.III (1972).[3]*

> *Apollo 11 (calling Mission Control): 'Those are giant things. No, no, no – this is not an optical illusion. No one is going to believe this! ... They're here under the surface ... We saw some visitors. They were here for a while, observing the instruments ... I say that there were other spaceships. They're lined up in the other side of the crater! ...They've landed here. There they are and they're watching us ...' Ancient Alien Ancestors (2017).[4]*

This was taken to mean two large mysterious flying objects that had landed on the rim of a crater near the Moon module, and were watching from the lunar surface.

There have also been claims by the former chief of NASA communications specialists who was one of the scientists who conceived and designed Apollo spacecraft.

Not only had this Apollo mission been observed during the lunar landing by unidentified flying objects,[5] but also that '... all Apollo and Gemini flights were followed, both at a distance and sometimes quite closely, by extraterrestrial space vehicles – flying saucers, or UFOs...'[6]

The last manned lunar mission of the Apollo Program was in 1972. Further exploration of other planets by NASA conducted only by unmanned probes followed, with reusable manned space shuttles for routine access

Figure 44: Space Explorer (© Shutterstock)

into space being introduced from 1981.

By 2000, the International Space Station provided the permanent human presence in space originally sought after the concept of establishing a base on the Moon had been abandoned.[7]

Perhaps the most salient legacy of our lunar landings and the ongoing debate surrounding the likelihood of extraterrestrial visitors was the inscription on the plaque left on the Moon by Apollo 11:

> *Here Men From Planet Earth*
> *First Set Foot Upon The Moon*
> *July 1969 A.D.*
> *We Came In Peace For All Mankind* [8]

What will become of *Homo sapiens* as we venture further away from our solar system in future centuries? It would seem that we will probably be inextricably linked to what extraterrestrial life-forms are eventually encountered, and presumably they may be quite diverse.

EXTRATERRESTRIAL

Aside from finding suitable habitable exoplanets like our own, we may encounter alien life so different and so much more advanced as to be almost incomprehensible.

If it is an alien civilisation comprising a society of individuals like Earth, will it also comprise synthetically intelligent androids as compliant servers or beings that have evolved with superior intelligence?

Extraterrestrial life could be so advanced as to be a single integrated intelligence, or perhaps so sophisticated individuals are able to control their physical appearances and their consciousness at will so we cannot detect or recognise them.[9]

Might such alien life be entirely incompatible with organic beings?

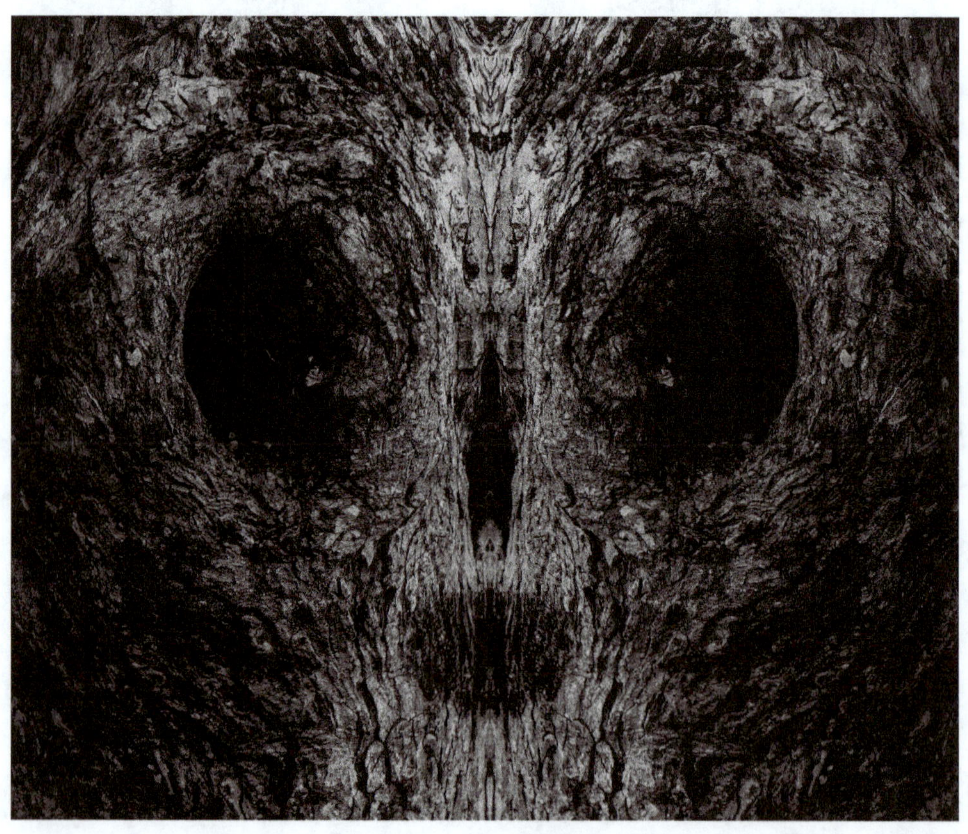

Figure 45: Just Part of the Furniture (© Shutterstock)

Would we simply become part of an existing galactic community of alien life-forms once our technology and capabilities permit us to find them? Another daunting but unlikely possibility is that our planet is actually unique in the cosmos and the centre for establishment of organic beings. Being alone in such a busy galaxy is surely not such a great outcome for our species.

It may appear obvious for space exploration, but receiving and decoding alien signals from other worlds, and responding appropriately, could be the most important element to our future development.

If we cannot detect or decipher the messages they might be transmitting, how can we respond and confirm our presence? There certainly is a long journey of discovery and learning ahead for our civilisation, given there are far more unanswered questions than suitable answers provided.

Look not across the universe but within oneself to discover what humans are capable of achieving in the exploration of the vast expanses of space and the life-forms that may exist there.

EPILOGUE

Twenty years from now you will be more disappointed by the things you didn't do than by the ones you did do. So throw off the bowlines. Sail away from the safe harbor. Catch the trade winds in your sails. Explore. Dream. Discover.[1]

H.Jackson Brown Jr., *P.S. I Love You (1990)*

'A spaceship is created from pure energy into physical substance, and we do this in space. The material of the spaceship's outer skin is completely smooth without rivets; the material is created in one piece in a continuously circular shape. The radius of the curvature transforms the total mass of the spaceship's outer skin into a combination of matter and anti-matter, as the atomic creation of the outer skin is conductive to energizing in alternate pulses.'[2]

This convoluted yet highly technical explanation of the fundamentals in creating an alien spaceship was reportedly relayed to a South African woman through her telepathic contact with an extraterrestrial life-force, and subsequently published in her 1980 autobiography of such extraordinary experiences.

This revealing and imaginative insight into the construction of a sophisticated alien spacecraft for interstellar travel utilising the cosmic energy from planetary atmospheres for its propulsion is possibly a succinct vision into our own likely future of space travel.

It may constitute scientific fantasy in the realms of unproven technologies today, but it does provide us with an intriguing and valuable insight as to what may be achievable elsewhere in our universe.

If there really are extraterrestrials, are we listening to their messages?

Extraterrestrial life may not only be observing and investigating our civil-

Figure 46: Them (© Shutterstock)

isations, but also cautiously supplying subtle communication signals from time to time.

One such common theme appears to be the importance and progress of our human development. Are we ready to embrace far more advanced technological life-forms who have already conquered space and time travel? Should we be expanding our mental consciousness far beyond our present capabilities to sufficiently stimulate our progress?

Significantly, can our species overcome a formidable fear of the emptiness of our universe and its billions of stars? When we have overcome these fears, then it will be time to join our interstellar neighbours.

'I'm not afraid of the dark I know. It's the dark I don't that terrifies me.'[3]

REFERENCES

CHAPTER 1: The Mysterions

1. Williams, Matt, '10 Interesting Facts About The Milky Way', 19 September 2017 (as updated from original 3 December 2014), *Universe Today*, https://www.universetoday.com/22285/facts-about-the-milky-way/, Accessed 13 August 2018.

2. Martialay, Mary, 'The Corrugated Galaxy – Milky Way May Be Much Larger Than Previously Estimated', 11 March 2015, *RPI News, Rensselaer Polytechnic Institute*, Archived from original on 13 August 2018.

3. Sagan and Page, 'The Extraterrestrial and Other Hypotheses', in *UFO's – A Scientific Debate*, 1972, p.274.

4. Wikipedia encyclopedia, 'List of interstellar radio messages', 17 July 2018, https://en.wikipedia.org/wiki/List_of_interstellar_radio_messages, Accessed 13 August 2018.

5. CBS, 'To Serve Man', in *The Twilight Zone: The Original Series (1959-1964)*, Season 3, Episode 24, originally aired 2 March 1962, https://en.wikipedia.org/wiki/ To_Serve_Man.

6. Dunning, Brian, 'Skeptoid #342: Was the Wow! Signal Alien?', 25 December 2012, https://skeptoid.com/episodes/4342, Skeptoid accessed 14 August 2018.

7. ibid., Dunning, 2012.

8. Verma, 'The mystery of the 'Wow' signal', in *Why Aren't They Here?* 2008, pp.143-4.

9. Ancient Maya Civilization, Updated July 2018, www.yucatanadventure.com.mx/maya_civilization.htm#THE_GREAT_MAYAN_SACRED_

TREE_OF_LIFE:__LA_CEIBA_ Accessed 5 October 2018.

10. Mark, Joshua J., 'Pacal's Sarcophagus and Identity Controversy', in *K'inich_Janaab'_Pakal, Ancient History Encyclopedia*, 28 March 2014, https://www.ancient.eu/Kinich_Janaab_Pacal/ Retrieved 8 October 2018.

11. Noone, Alex, 'King of the stars?', in *Were the Mayans ancient aliens?*, 23 February 2018, https://www.lifedeathprizes.com/amazing-stuff/ mayans-ancient-aliens-11094 Retrieved 5 October 2018.

CHAPTER 2: The Beginning

1.Papagiannis, Michael, L., 'The Search For Extraterrestrial Technologies In Our Solar System', in Vol.74, *Progress in the Search for Extraterrestrial Life Conference*, Astronomical Society of the Pacific, 1993, p.425.

2. Haze, X., 'Chapter 1 – Planet 9 From Outer Space', in *Ancient Aliens in the Bible: Evidence of UFOs, Nephilim, and the True Face of Angels in Ancient Scriptures*, 2017, p.11.

3. ibid., p.12.

4. Haze, op. cit., 'Adams And Eves In Laboratories', p.19.

5. Mowaljarlai and Malnic, 'Creation in the Kimberley', in *Yorro Yorro*, 1993, pp.132-37.

6. Flood, 'The Kimberley', in *Rock art of the dreamtime: images of ancient Australia*, 1997, p.296.

7. Blundell and Woolagoodja, *Keeping the Wanjinas Fresh: Sam Woolagoodja and the enduring power of Lalai*, 2005, p.23.

8. Grant and Greenop, *The Handbook of Contemporary Indigenous Architecture*, Footnote 21, p.69.

9. Flood, op.cit., pp.296-8.

10. AHC, 'Human Arrivals, in *Final Assessment of National Heritage Values of the West Kimberley: Description and History – One Place, Many Stories*, 2011, p.15.

11. Mowaljarlai and Malnic, op.cit., p.133.

12. Ryan and Akerman, *Images of Power*, 1993, p.12.

13. Mowaljarlai and Malnic, op,cit., p.200.

14. ibid.

15. ibid., p.198.

16. Anderson, Mike, *A Civilization without Cities?*   6 February 2010, http://www.mikeanderson.biz/2010/02/civilization-without-cities.html. Accessed 24 September 2018.

17. Hart, 'Egypt: Civilization without Cities?', in *Ancient Alien Ancestors*, 2017, p.80.

18. Hart, op.cit., 'Alien Message in Stone', pp.42-4.

19. Smith, Craig B., 'Project Management B.C.', in *Civil Engineering Magazine*, June 1999, p.2.

20. Hart, op.cit., p.46.

21. Smith, op.cit., p.3.

22. ibid.

23. Hart, op.cit., pp.76-7, p.85.

24. ibid., pp.84-5.

25. Hart, op.cit., 'The Giza Pyramids Represent the Three Inner Planets', p.94.

26. Smith, op.cit., p.6.

CHAPTER 3: Spacecraft

1. United States Air Force, 'Definitions', in *Air Force Regulation 200-2 (or AFR 200-2), Unidentified Flying Objects Reporting*, 26 August 1953 & Amendment 200-2A, Superceded 12 August 1954, p.1.

2. Sagan and Page, op.cit., p.12.

3. Danelek, 'Lenticular Clouds', in *UFOs The Great Debate*, 2008, p.69.

4. Hamblyn, 'Strange Shapes', in *Extraordinary Clouds*, 2009, p.54.

5. Danelek, 'Project Blue Book and the Condon Report', pp.99-100.

6. Sagan and Page, op.cit., p.298.

7. MacDonald, James, 'UFOs – An International Scientific Problem', presented at Astronautics Symposium, Canadian Aeronautics and Space Institute,Montreal, Canada, 12 March 1968.http://www.project1947.com/articles/casia_68.htm.

8. Sparks, Brad, 'BB Case Statistics and Problems', in *Comprehensive Catalog of 1,700 Project Blue Book UFO Unknowns*, Version 1.26, 31 January 2016, p.3. www.cufos.org/pdfs/BB_Unknowns-1.26.pdf

9. Sagan and Page, op.cit., p.297.

10. They Tailed a Saucer 86 miles! *Record-Courier*, Issue 18 April 1966, Ravenna, Ohio. www.nicap.org/images/raven18.gif. Accessed 21 August 2018.

11. Portage County Ohio UFO Chase, 17 April 1966, Ravenna Ohio, *National Investigations Committee on Aerial Phenomena*, Accessed 21 August 2018.

12. Davenport, Peter and Geremia, Peter, 'Exeter (New Hampshire) sightings', in *The Mammoth Encyclopedia of Extraterrestrial Encounters*, 2012.

13. Muscarello, Norman J., '1965 Witness Statement', in *The Hynek UFO Report*, 1977, p.158.

14. McGaha, James and Nickell, Joe, 'Exeter Incident' Solved! A Classic UFO Case. Forty-Five Years 'Cold', *Skeptical Inquirer*, Vol. 35-6, November/December 2011, https://www.csicop.org/si/show/exeter_incident_solved_a_classic_ufo_case_forty-five_years_cold, Accessed 22 August 2018.

15. ibid.

16. Sparks, op.cit., Catalog Item 997, p.187.

17. Rodgers, Bruce A., 'UFOs: Their Performance Characteristics', in *UFO Investigator*, 1973, p.2. http://cufos.org/UFOI_and_Selected_Documents/UFOI/093%20DECEMBER%201973.pdf

18. Hill, 'What's a Good Name?', in *Unconventional Flying Objects*, 1995, pp. 26-7.

CHAPTER 4: Wingless Shapes and Nocturnal Lights

1. Bennett, J., 'Worlds Beyond Imagination', in *Beyond UFOs*, 2008, p.15

2. Danelek, op.cit.,p.76.

3. Hill, op.cit., 'Performance:Speed', p.15.

4. Thompson, Elvia, Henry, Keith and Williams, Leslie, 'Faster Than a Speeding Bullet: Guinness Recognizes NASA Scramjet', in *NASA News*, 20 June 2005, Retrieved 4 October 2018.

5. Hill. op.cit., p.312, p.328.

6. Twinning, Nathan, General. Command Headquarters, *Air Materiel Command Opinion Concerning "Flying Discs" Memorandum*, *U-39552*, 23 September 1947, www.majesticdocuments.com/pdf/

twiningopinionamc_23sept47.pdf, Accessed 23 August 2018.

7. ibid.

8. Chung, Frank, 'The only man to ever shoot at a UFO', in News.com.au 30 December 2015. https://www.news.com.au/finance/work/leaders/the-only-man-to-ever-shoot-at-a-ufo/news-story/8fdf6eddbe5363fb5823f1625 a7713f5 11 October 2018.

9. Sagan and Page, op.cit., p.xxv.

10. Danelek, 'Experimental Military Aircraft', op.cit., pp.76-7.

11. British Ministry of Defence, 'Study Method', in *Unidentified Aerial Phenomena in the UK Air Defence Region: Executive Summary*, 2000, p.5.

12. ibid., 'Key Supporting Findings', pp.6-7.

13. ibid., p.7.

14. ibid.

15. Watkins, Eli and Todd, Brian, Former Pentagon UFO official: 'We may not be alone', CNN Politics, Updated 19 December 2017, https://edition.cnn.com/2017/12/18/politics/luis-elizondo-ufo-pentagon/index.html, Retrieved 28 August 2018.

16. Danelek, 'Conclusions - Alternative UFO Theories', op.cit., p.57.

CHAPTER 5: Landings

1. Dartnell, Lewis, '(Un)welcome Visitors: Why Aliens Might Visit Us', in *Aliens*, 2016, pp.26-31.

2. Sparks, op.cit., www.cufos.org/pdfs/BB_Unknowns-1.26.pdf

3. Sagan, *Pale Blue Dot: A Vision of the Human Future in Space*, 1994, and part of commencement address delivered on 11 May 1996.

4. Birnes, 'Trace Evidence', in *The Everything UFO Book*, 2012, p.76.

5. Austin, Jon, ' I have PROVED an ALIEN UFO landed on Earth, *Express UK*, Issue 6 February 2017, https://www.express.co.uk/news/weird/763816/UFO-landed-earth-proof-Delphos-Dr-Erol-Faruk Accessed 25 September 2018.

6. Faruk, *The Compelling Scientific Evidence for UFOs*, 2014.

7. ibid.

8. Birnes, op,cit., pp.76-7.

9. ibid.

10. Faruk, Erol, 'The Delphos Case: Soil Analysis and Appraisal of a CE-2 Report' in *Journal of UFO Studies, New Series, vol.1*, 1989, pp.41-66.

11. Budinger, Phyllis, 'Case File: Analysis of Soil Samples Related to the Delphos, Kansas, 2 November 1971', in *The Phyllis Budinger Collection*, 1999, http://www.theblackvault.com/casefiles/analysis-soil-samples-related-delphos-kansas-november-2-1971/ Accessed 28 September 2018.

12. Faruk, op.cit., *The Compelling Scientific Evidence for UFOs*.

13. Birnes, op.cit., pp.77-8.

14. Hill, op. cit., p.17.

15. ibid., pp.13-4.

CHAPTER 6: Visitors

1. Verma, op. cit., 'What would aliens really look like?', pp. 199-200.

2. Cobb, Mathew, 'Alone in the Universe: The Improbability of Alien Civilisations', in *Aliens*, 2016, p.156.

3. Birnes, 'The Incredible Mac Magruder Story', in *UFO Magazine, Vol.21, No.4*, June 2006, p.34.

4. Birnes, 'Wright Field and Marion Magruder', in *Everything UFO Book*, 2012, p.39.

5. Birnes, 'The Incredible Mac Magruder Story', p.35, p.38.

6. Birnes, *Everything UFO Book*, p.39.

7. Verma, op,cit.,'Lithopanspermia', p.58.

8. ibid.,'Mars-Earth panspermia', p.65.

9. Hart, op.cit., 'Cosmic Seeds of Life', pp.12-13, p.17.

10. ibid., p.12.

11. Savage, Hartsfield and Salisbury, 'Meteorite Yields Evidence of Primitive Life on Early Mars', Press Release 96-160, 7 August 1996, *NASA Johnson Space Centre and Stanford University*, https://www2.jpl.nasa.gov/snc/nasa1.html, Accessed 4 September 2018

12. Wasowicz, Lidia, 'Bacteria awakened after 250 million years', *United Press International Science Archives*, 20 February 2000, https://www.upi.com/Archives/2000/10/20/Bacteria-awakened-after-250-million-years/6668972014400/, Accessed 3 September 2018.

CHAPTER 7: Alien Innovation

1. Birnes, 'Element 115', in *The Everything UFO Book*, 2012, p.163

2. ibid., p.161.

3. Tracey Walter ('Miller'), *Repo Man*, Sci-Fi Film, Alex Cox (Dir,) Edge City, Universal Pictures, USA, 1984.

4. White *et al*, 'Measurement of Impulsive Thrust from a Closed Radio-Frequency Cavity in Vacuum', in *Journal of Propulsion and Power, Vol. 33, No. 4*, July-August 2017, pp.830-41.

5. Behrendt, Kenneth, 'The Anti-Mass Field Generator', in *Anti-Gravity and the Unified Field*, 1990, p.134.

6. McFadden, Johnjoe, 'Quantum Leap: Could Quantum Mechanics Hold The Secret of (Alien) Life?', in *Aliens*, 2016, p.137.

7. Pope *et al*, 'Strange Symbols', in *Encounter in Rendlesham Forest*, 2014, pp.6-8.

8. Bruni, 'Evidence of Jim Penniston', in *You Can't Tell The People* (Ebook), 2001, ref. 1.

9. 'The Rendlesham Forest Incident – Craft of Unknown Origin', in *Pictorial Glyphs*. www.therendleshamforestincident.com/Pictoral_Glyphs.html Accessed 14 October 2018.

10. Pope *et al*, op.cit., pp.6-8.

11. Luciano, Joe, 'Written Statement by Jim Penniston concerning Rendlesham Forest Binary Code', in *The Decoded Binary Code*, www.therendleshamforestincident.com/The_Decoded_Binary_Code.html Retrieved 14 October 2018.

12. Luciano, Joe, *The Decoded Binary Code*, Accessed 14 October 2018.

13. Pictorial Glyphs, op.cit., 14 October 2018.

CHAPTER 8: Are We Alone?

1. Bennett, J., 'What I Know About Aliens', in *Beyond UFOs: The Search for Extraterrestrial Life and its Astonishing Implications for Our Future*, 2008, p.57.

2. ibid., 'Where Is Everybody?' pp.282-3.

3. ibid., p.284.

4. ibid., p.285.

5. Schneider, J. 'Interactive Extra-solar Planets Catalog', in *The*

Extrasolar Planets Encyclopedia, exoplanet.eu/catalog/, Retrieved 30 August 2018.

6. Dole, *Habitable Planets for Man*, 1964.

7. Landau, E.,'New clues to compositions of TRAPPIST-1 planets', *Exoplanet Exploration*, NASA's Jet Propulsion Laboratory, California Institute of Technology, 5 February 2018. https://exoplanets.nasa.gov/news/1481/new-clues-to-compositions-of-trappist-1-planets/ Accessed 31 August 2018.

8. Mitnick, R., 'From ESO: TRAPPIST-1 Planets Probably Rich in Water', *Sciencesprings*, 6 February 2018, https://sciencesprings.wordpress.com/2018/02/05/from-eso-trappist-1-planets-probably-rich-in-water/, Accessed 31 August 2018.

9. Cooper, K., 'TRAPPIST-1 exoplanets could harbour significant amounts of water', *physicsworld*: Planetary Science, 13 February 2018, https://physicsworld.com/a/trappist-1-exoplanets-could-harbour-significant-amounts-of-water/ Retrieved 31 August 2018.

10. ibid.

11. Strickland, Ashley,'Closest potentially habitable planet to our solar system found', *CNN Space+Science*, Updated 25 August 2016, https://edition.cnn.com/2016/08/24/health/proxima-b-centauri-rocky-planet-habitable-zone-neighbor-star/, Accessed 11 September 2018.

12.'Planet in star system nearest our Sun 'may have oceans'', *Phys.Org. Astronomy*, 6 October 2016, https://phys.org/news/2016-10-planet-star-nearest-sun-oceans.html, Accessed 11 September 2018.

13. ibid.

14. Bennett, op,cit., 'What is Life?', p.82.

15. Rees, Martin, 'Aliens and Us: Could Post-humans Spread through the Galaxy?', in *Aliens*, 2016, p.17.

CHAPTER 9: Incursions

1. BBC, 'Silence in the Library', in *Doctor Who*, Series 4, Episode 8, originally aired 31 May 2008. Retrieved 7 September 2018.

2. Godwin, 'You Make The Call', in *True UFO Accounts: From the Vaults of FATE Magazine*, 2011, pp.271-2.

3. ibid., pp.273-4.

4. Barker, Gray, 'The Monster and the Saucer -January 1953', in *True UFO Accounts: From the Vaults of FATE Magazine*, p.108.
5. ibid., p.109.
6. ibid., p.105.
7. ibid., p.107.
8. Birnes, 'The Alan Godfrey Abduction', in *The Everything UFO Book*, pp.90-1.
9. ibid., p.93.
10. Dillon, Jonathon, 'Former policeman's encounter with a UFO pulls crowds', in *Lancashire Telegraph*, Issue 21 October 2014, https://www.lancashiretelegraph.co.uk/news/11548976.Former_policeman_s_story_of_a_close_encounter_with_a_UFO_pulls_in_crowds/ Accessed 30 September 2018.
11. Birnes, op.cit., p.95.
12. Hill, op.cit., pp.18-9.

CHAPTER 10: Universal Biosignatures

1. Verma, op.cit.,'Listening to the 'songs' of the cosmos', p.150.
2. ibid., 'What would aliens really look like?', p.201.
3. CBS, 'Probe 7, Over and Out', in *The Twilight Zone: The Original Series (1959-1964)*, Season 5, Episode 9, originally aired 29 November 1963.
4. CBS, op.cit., Closing Narration, https://en.wikipedia.org/wiki/Probe_7,_Over_and_Out, Retrieved 18 September 2018.

CHAPTER 11: Our Astral Destiny

1. Hart, op.cit.,'Enigmas of the Space Program', pp.238-9.
2. Schelly, 'A New Life', in *Otto Binder: The Life and Work of a Comic Book and Science Fiction Visionary*, 2016, pp.249-250.
3. Binder, Otto, 'Secret Messages from UFOs', in *Saga's UFO Special, Vol.III*, 1972, p.46.
4. Hart, op,cit., pp.237-8.
5. Chatelain, 'The Apollo Spacecraft', in *Our Ancestors Came From Outer Space*, 1978, p.17.
6. ibid., p.16.

7. Hart, op.cit., p.240.

8. NASA, EP-72 Log of Apollo 11 (20 July 1969 Transcript).

9. Rees, op.cit., pp.20-21.

CHAPTER 12: Epilogue

1. Brown Jr., *P.S. I Love You.* 1990, p.13.

2. Klarer, *Beyond the Light Barrier*, 1980, p.47.

3. Foster, *Alien: The Official Movie Novelization*, 1979, Chp II.

BIBLIOGRAPHY

Al-Khalili, Jim (ed.), *Aliens: The World's Leading Scientists on the Search for Extraterrestrial Life*, Profile Books, Great Britain, 2016.

Astronomical Society of the Pacific Conference Series, Vol.74, *Progress in the Search for Extraterrestrial Life*, Santa Cruz, California, 16-20 August, 1993, G.Seth Shostak (ed.), Astronomical Society of the Pacific, San Francisco, 1995.

Australian Heritage Council (AHC), *Final Assessment of National Heritage Values of the West Kimberley: Description and History – One Place, Many Stories*, Department of the Environment and Energy, Australian Government, 2011.

Bennett, Jeffrey, *Beyond UFOs: The Search for Extraterrestrial Life and its Astonishing Implications for Our Future*, Princeton University Press, Princeton, USA and Oxford, UK, 2008.

Birnes, William J., *UFO Magazine, Vol.21, No,1*, Vicky Cooper, Los Angeles, USA, June 2006.

Birnes, William J., *The Everything UFO Book: An investigation of sightings, cover-ups, and the quest for extraterrestrial life*, F+W Media Inc., Avon, Massachusetts, USA, 2012.

Blundell, Valda and Woolagoodja, Donny, *Keeping the Wanjinas Fresh: Sam Woolagoodja and the enduring power of Lalai*, Fremantle Arts Centre Press, Fremantle, Australia, 2005.

BME, *Civil Engineering Magazine, Vol.69, No. 6*, Department of Construction Technology and Management, June 1999.

EXTRATERRESTRIAL

British Ministry of Defence, *Unidentified Aerial Phenomena in the UK Air Defence Region: Executive Summary*, Scientific and Technical Memorandum No 55/2/00, Defence Intelligence Staff, London, December 2000.

Brown, Harriett Jackson, *P.S. I Love You: When Mom wrote she always saved the best for last*, Rutledge Hill Press, USA, 1990.

Bruni, Georgini, *You Can't Tell The People: The Cover-Up of Britain's Roswell*, Pan Books, London, 2001.

Chatelain, Maurice, *Our Ancestors Came From Outer Space: A NASA Expert Confirms Mankinds Extraterrestrial Origins*, Doubleday, New York, 1978.

Childress, David Hatcher (ed.), *Anti-Gravity and the Unified Field*, Adventures Unlimited Press, Illinois, USA, 1990.

Danelek, Jeffrey Allan, *UFOs The Great Debate: An Objective Look at Extraterrestrials, Government Cover-Ups, and the Prospect of First Contact*, 1st Ed., Llewellyn Publications, Minnesota, USA, 2008.

Dole, Stephen H., *HABITABLE PLANETS for Man*, 1st Ed., Blaisdale Publishing Company, New York, Toronto, London, 1964.

Faruk, Erol A., *The Compelling Scientific Evidence for UFOs: The Analysis of the Delphos, Kansas UFO Landing Report*, CreateSpace Independent Publishing, November 2014.

Flood, Josephine, *Rock art of the Dreamtime: images of ancient Australia*, Angus and Robertson, Pymble, New South Wales, 1997.

Foster, Alan Dean, *Alien™: The Official Movie Novelization*, Titan Books, London, United Kingdom, 2014.

Godwin, David, *True UFO Accounts: From the Vaults of FATE Magazine, 60 Years of Close Encounters*, Llewellyn Publications, Woodbury, Minnesota, USA, 2011.

Good, Timothy, *Above Top Secret: The Worldwide U.F.O. Cover-up*, Quill William Morrow, New York, 1988.

Goodrich, Richelle E., *Smile Anyway:Quotes, Verse, and Grumblings for*

Every Day of the Year, CreateSpace Independent Publishing Platform, 2015.

Grant, Elizabeth, Greenop, Kelly, Refiti, Albert and Glenn, Danie (eds.), *The Handbook of Contemporary Indigenous Architecture*, Springer, Singapore, 2018.

Grimm, S., *et al*, The nature of the TRAPPIST-1 exoplanets, ESO 1805, *Astronomy and Astrophysics Journal*, 2018.

Hamblyn, Richard, *Extraordinary Clouds: Skies of the unexpected from the beautiful to the bizarre*, David & Charles, Cincinnati, Ohio, USA, 2009.

Hart, Will, *Ancient Alien Ancestors: Advanced Technologies That Terraformed Our World*, Bear & Company, Rochester, Vermont, USA, 2017.

Haze, Xaviant, *Ancient Aliens in the Bible: Evidence of UFOs, Nephilim, and the True Face of Angels in Ancient Scriptures*, E-book, Career Press, USA, 2017.

Hill, Paul R., *Unconventional Flying Objects: A Former NASA Scientist Explains How UFOs Really Work*, Hampton Roads Publishing Company, Virginia, USA, 1995.

Hynek, J.Allen, *The Hynek UFO Report*, Dell, New York, 1977.

Klarer, Elizabeth, *Beyond the Light Barrier*, Howard Timms, Aylesbury, United Kingdom, 1980.

Knight, Damon, *Galaxy Science Fiction*, Issue November, 1950, Galaxy Publishing Corporation, USA, 1950.

Lovecraft, H.P., *The Colour Out of Space*, *Amazing Stories*, Experimenter Publishing, USA, September 1927.

McDonald, James E., *UFOs – an international scientific problem*, Astronautics Symposium, Canadian Aeronautics and Space Institute, Montreal, Canada, 12 March 1968.

McDonald, James E., *Statement on Unidentified Flying Objects submitted to the House Committee on Science and Astronautics*, Symposium on

EXTRATERRESTRIAL

Unidentified Flying Objects, Washington, USA, 29 July 1968.

McDonald, James E., *Science in Default: Twenty-Two Years of Inadequate UFO Investigations*, AAAS 134th Meeting, Tucson, Arizona, 27 December 1969.

Mowaljarlai, David and Malnic, Judy, *Yorro Yorro =everything standing up alive: Spirit of the Kimberley*, Magabala Books, Broome, Western Australia, 1993.

National Investigations Committee on Aerial Phenomena (NICAP), *UFO Investigator*, Kensington, Maryland, USA, December 1973.

Pope, Nick, Penniston, Jim and Burroughs, John, *Encounter in Rendlesham Forest: The Inside Story of the World's Best-Documented UFO Incident*, 1st Ed., Thomas Dunne Books, St Martin's Press, New York, USA, 2014.

Ryan, Judith with Akerman, Kim, *Images of Power: Aboriginal Art of the Kimberley*, National Gallery of Victoria, Melbourne, 1993.

Sagan, Carl and Page Thornton (eds.), *UFO's – A Scientific Debate*, Cornell University Press, Ithaca and London, 1972.

Sagan, Carl, *Cosmos: A Personal Voyage*, 1st Ed., Random House, New York, 1980.

Sagan, Carl, *Pale Blue Dot: A Vision of the Human Future in Space*, 1st Ed., Random House, New York, USA, 1994.

Schelly, Bill, *Otto Binder: The Life and Work of a Comic Book and Science Fiction Visionary*, North Atlantic Books, Berkeley, California, USA, 2016.

Singer, Martin, M. (ed.), *Saga's UFO Special, Vol.III*, Gambi Publications, Brooklyn, New York, 1972.

Streicher, Thomas James, *Extra-Planetary Experiences: Alien-Human Contact and the Expansion of Consciousness*, Bear & Company, Vermont, USA, 2012.

Story, Ronald (ed.), *The Mammoth Encyclopedia of Extraterrestrial Encounters: The Definitive Illustrated A-Z Guide To All Things Alien*,

EBook, Robinson, New York, 2012.

Swords, Michael D. (ed.), *Journal of UFO Studies, New Series, Vol.1*, The J.Allen Hynek Center for UFO Studies, Chicago, USA, 1989.

Verma, Surendra, *Why Aren't They Here?:The Question of Life on Other Worlds*, Icon Books,Cambridge, UK, 2008.

White, Harold; March, Paul; Lawrence, James;Vera, Jerry; Sylvester, Andre; Brady, David and Bailey, Paul, *Measurement of Impulsive Thrust from a Closed Radio-Frequency Cavity in Vacuum, NASA Johnson Space Centre, Journal of Propulsion and Power, Vol. 33, No. 4*, July-August 2017.

Wilson, Don, *Our Mysterious Spaceship Moon*, 1st Ed., Dell Publishing, New York, 1975.

Wilson, Don, *Secrets Of Our Mysterious Spaceship Moon*, 1st Ed., Dell Publishing, New York, 1979.

ABOUT THE AUTHOR

Figure 47: The Sign (© Shutterstock)

Simon King is an emerging Australian author who has published six books:

Crocodiles and Cocktails: A Decade of Adventure at the Kimberley Frontier

Witchcraft, Whispers, Shadows and Strange Sights: A Journey into the Unknown and Unexpected

Marbles, Marella Jubes and Milk Bottles: My Golden Years of Australian Childhood

Robot Awakening: The Time of Artificial Life

On The Edge: Extreme Life

Acetylene Dreams: Far Beyond

Each book encompasses different aspects of life's journey, and engages many interesting historical and contemporary perspectives. His literary works can be reviewed on the website www.sdkauthor.com.

Simon's interest in exploring the potential existence of extraterrestrial life-forms is based upon the avid interest in science fiction he has had since childhood, and his research into the myriad of possibilities that extraterrestrials may present. This book provides some intriguing responses to such matters by attempting to unravel fact from fiction relevant to our own astral destiny within the known universe.